WITSEC BOOK FOUR

FREE ME

ASHLEY N. ROSTEK

FREE ME

Edited by Alexandra Fresch of To the Letter Services

Photography & Cover design by The Dirty Tease

Formatting by Savannah Richey of Peachy Keen Author Services

This is a work of fiction. All names, characters, places, and incidents are the product of the author's imagination or are used fictitiously. Any resemblance to actual persons, living or dead, organizations, events, or locals is purely coincidental.

BOOKS BY ASHLEY N. ROSTEK

WITSEC Series

Find Me

Save Me

Love Me

Free Me

The Maura Quinn Series

Embrace the Darkness

Endure the Pain

Endurance

Escape the Reaper

MR. X

She's as beautiful as I remember, I thought as I watched her walk out of school with her little friend, who had bright green and black hair. My Shiloh had colored hair as well. It was red like blood. It suited her. Blood had always suited her. Especially when it was smeared across her pale, soft skin.

Just envisioning it brought me back to the night I'd made myself her whole world. I had painted her with so much blood. Hers. Her sister's. She had shed such beautiful tears as I'd severed the ties that kept her from me. It had been the perfect night until she had acted like an ungrateful brat. I regretted losing my patience with her and punishing her like I had. After some time apart, I'd realized my mistake. I had forgotten that my Shiloh loved to play hard to get, loved to be chased.

I wouldn't make that mistake this time. I would do my best to be even more patient with her. No matter how tempting it was to just take what was mine, I would make our reunion better than perfect. Our reunion would make time stop moving. When we finally came together, every inch of her would be covered with blood and tears. I wanted my hands to slip over her skin when I buried my cock into her cunt. I needed her to be branded with bruises from gripping her too hard as I fucked her. I loved leaving evidence of my claim on her body. I could see one of my marks on her inner arm right now. To add more would be the fruit of all my labor.

RED AND BLUE LIGHTS LIT UP THE DARKENED neighborhood. My cheeks were wet and cold from the nonstop tears that rolled down them. Dried blood covered my hands and knees. Ethan's hysterical voice as the paramedics had rushed Isabelle out of his house was playing on repeat in my head, drowning out all the noise around me.

"What happened?" he demanded as he pushed through the crowd that had congregated in the foyer to watch the paramedics hurry Isabelle downstairs on a gurney.

I froze in my descent behind them on the stairs, my eyes locking on Ethan just as he realized who was being carried away. The widening of his green eyes and the horror and panic that filled them gutted me. I stopped breathing and tears blinded me as he rushed to her side with frantic words:

"Isabelle!"

"What happened?!"

"Who did this to her?!"

The ambulance had long since rushed off with Ethan

trailing it in his own car. Now I was standing in the middle of the street in front of Ethan's house, staring down the dark road as if I could still see the ambulance and Ethan speeding away. Police, crime-scene personnel, and a few people who had been attending Ethan's birthday party were moving around me. The police had finished taking my statement, but were still speaking to Keelan, Knox, and Creed.

The dried blood on my skin made it feel tight. I drew my hands up to stare at them. They were trembling. Strangely, the blood didn't trigger an episode. Maybe because I was already standing in hell, a new level that my mind would no doubt drag me back to later.

Staring at my hands, I hated how familiar the sight was. The smell, too. The pungent scent of pennies had been embedded in my nose since Keelan and I had found Isabelle, butchered and barely alive in one of the bathrooms in Ethan's house.

He had found me.

You are mine. X.

He had written it in Isabelle's blood—a message for me on the bathroom mirror, because he knew I'd find her.

A sob barreled its way up my throat.

Oh, Isabelle.

The guilt and sorrow were so heavy that my chest felt moments from caving in. My body demanded that I just curl up and cry. That demand nearly made my knees buckle. I fought it, though.

Fisting my bloody hands, I dropped them back at my sides and closed my tear-filled eyes.

I'm sorry, Isabelle.

I'm so, so sorry.

I wished I could have gone to the hospital with Ethan—to be there for Isabelle and him.

But I couldn't.

I had to put distance between me and them. Even now, I could feel *him* watching. And if I stayed here, he'd go after Ethan next, and then someone closer to me.

Maybe he already has.

I glanced at Knox, Keelan, and Creed. Colt's absence made my heart pound painfully in my chest. I hadn't had a chance to speak to Knox and Creed since Keelan and I'd split up from them to search for Colt around Ethan's house, but I'd overheard Knox tell Keelan, just as EMS had rushed into the bathroom to help Isabelle, that he and Creed hadn't found Colt.

The thought of Mr. X taking Colt terrified me so much that I felt like I was going to vomit.

I inhaled deeply through my nose and exhaled long and slow through my mouth as I stared back down the street in the direction the ambulance had driven.

I couldn't let what I was feeling consume me. Not right now. Not with so much at stake. I had to bury it. To survive. To find Colt. I had to. I'd done it before.

I can do it again.

With one last deep breath, I felt like I had a little more control of myself. Determination and understanding of what needed to be done began to take over.

I reached into my pocket and pulled out my personal phone. My burner phone was in the car in my purse. At this point, it didn't matter what phone I used. Mr. X had already found me. After tapping on Logan's contact, I brought the phone to my ear. It rang once and went to voicemail.

I walked farther away from the guys so I wouldn't be overheard. "I don't know if you're not answering because you're upset with me or you're dead. I'm praying it's the former." My voice was hollow, as if I'd been too successful in burying my emotions. "Mr. X has found me. Feel free to tell me *I told you so* the next time you see me. It's what I deserve. I'm a selfish piece of shit." I squeezed the phone. I didn't have time to wallow in guilt. "When you get this, I won't have this phone anymore. I'm going to do what you taught me. I'm going to get somewhere safe. Don't come looking for me. Just please focus on finding him. Just find him and kill him, Logan. Because if you don't..." A little bit of anguish seeped into my voice. I took in a calming breath to compose myself. I glanced at my guys again. The three of them were watching me as they spoke to the police. It was as if they were afraid to take their eyes off of me. "I'm terrified. I'm more terrified than I've ever been. It's not just me anymore." Maybe it was because I already knew what it was like to lose everything, and that knowledge...I wouldn't wish it on anyone, but right now, that experience was the only thing fueling my determination to never endure it again. I looked away from my guys and I stared down the road where the red and blue lights from the police cars didn't reach, where it was dark, where *he* could easily be watching me from. I let my anger show. I hoped he saw it. For too long I had given him my fear, my pain. He relished it and it only added to his obsession. No more. "I won't let him take my family from me again." I meant it. I would do whatever I had to in order to keep them safe. "I love you, Logan."

I hung up, and just as I was about to put my phone back into my pocket, it began ringing.

Unknown number, the screen read.

Colt was why I didn't hesitate to answer. I squared my

shoulders, bracing myself as I brought the phone to my ear. "Hello?"

"Hello, Shiloh Pierce," a familiar male voice said. "Or should I say Shiloh McConnell."

The voice didn't belong to Mr. X.

"It seems you kept digging, Sheriff," I said, and for a moment I thought maybe, just maybe, Cassy's father was behind all of this. And for that brief slice of time, a little bit of relief slipped in. But just as that short moment came, the memory of being locked in that interrogation room alone with him ended it. He'd had me pinned and bent over the table, twisting my arm behind my back at a painful angle.

"Don't play dumb. I know they chased you through the woods. My daughter told me. They went after you and never came back. You did something to them. You did or he did."

He had said *he did*.

"I already knew who you were when I made that threat," he said as if proud of himself.

"Was it your digging that led Mr. X here?" I questioned.

"Xander Xenos. Also referred to by his students as Mr. X. That's what the police officer I spoke to said in Maryland, and that you used to be his student."

"How did you find out who I was?"

"It wasn't easy." The lightness in his voice told me he was happy that I'd asked. "Nearly impossible, actually. But the weak link that led me to learn everything about you was your uncle. My officers who pulled you over on your way to school told me they had to let you go because you had a U.S. Marshal in the car with you. That made me wonder what your connection was to him, and from there I got my answers."

"And how did you track down Mr. X?"

"Not everything needs to be revealed over the phone," he said.

Like I'd want to talk to you in person.

Frustrated, I raised my hand to rub my face. Remembering that it was covered in blood, I froze and fisted my hand instead. "Whatever you did to bring him here, just know that Gabe and Amber are more than likely dead."

The line went quiet long enough to make my heart beat a little faster. "For your sake, that better not be true." His voice was low and rumbled just enough to tell me that it had taken everything to keep his voice calm. "I have your boyfriend. Well, one of them anyway."

My stomach sank and my heart pounded painfully in my chest.

"If you want him back—"

"Alive," I snapped.

He huffed a laugh that lacked any humor. "He's alive."

"How do I know that?"

"I guess you'll have to find that out for yourself. That is, if you're the one to get here first." I could feel his evil glee through the phone. "I'm going to call your Mr. X next. You like to run, right? Let's make this a race."

Even though I was as still as a statue, everything beneath my skin was pure chaos.

"However, if you do decide to enter this race to rescue your beloved, there is one rule," he said.

It wasn't hard to guess what it was. "I have to come alone."

"Very good," he praised, making me grind my teeth. "If you break the rule, I'll kill Colt myself."

I didn't know how I was going to slip away from the guys, but I'd figure it out. "Fine. Where are you?"

"Desert Stone Fitness." As soon as he said it, he hung up.

"Who were you talking to?" a voice asked.

I spun on my heels. Creed was right behind me and Knox and Keelan were walking over.

"Logan," I lied as a plan formed in my head. "He wants us to meet him back at your house."

All three of them frowned and I could see the doubt in their eyes.

I need to lie better. Colt's life depends on it.

"He's back?" Knox asked.

"Yes," I said as I pulled my keys from my pocket and stepped in the direction of my 4Runner. "We should go."

Keelan reached to take my keys. "Why don't I drive?"

I snapped my hand out of his reach and internally winced. "I—I need something to focus on."

Understanding, Keelan dropped his hand and nodded.

"Your hands are covered in blood," Knox said as he stared at me with an intense look that felt like he could see every lie that spilled from my lips.

I didn't want to hand over my keys, but I didn't have time to waste arguing. "Right." I gave the keys to Keelan before taking off toward my car. They thankfully followed.

"What about Colt?" Creed asked as we all climbed into my 4Runner.

I climbed into the backseat with him while Knox and Keelan sat up front. "Logan will help us find him." I hated lying—giving them false hope. And if I failed to save Colt...I didn't think I'd ever be able to forgive myself.

I couldn't afford to think like that right now. I needed to stay focused because I was undoubtedly walking into a trap. Maybe Sheriff McAllister wanted to hand me over to Mr. X, or follow through on his threat to kill me and make it look like a suicide. I had a gut feeling the former was what I was going to face. One twisted assurance I had was that Mr. X wouldn't allow the sheriff to kill me. In Mr. X's eyes, I belonged to him. Only he had the right to inflict my torture —my agony—and Jacob, Amber, and Gabe had made themselves a threat to that right. I was also sure Mr. X had twisted the situation in his head such that getting rid of them was his way of protecting me. It was why he'd left Jacob's body on my couch like a gift or like proof, as if to say, *This is what I'd do for you.* I wouldn't be surprised if the sheriff and Cassy found themselves missing next. Honestly, I was surprised the sheriff wasn't gone already. He posed the biggest threat to me.

Whatever the reason that kept the sheriff and Cassy out of Mr. X's reach, he had deemed the board cleared of enough obstacles to come after me. He felt like a shark circling me and the connections I had made. I had no idea how long he'd been circling, but he clearly had decided to get to me by going through those I cared about. He'd started with Isabelle. He probably planned to go after Ethan next. Who would be after that? Logan? He would save my guys for last. I knew that with every fiber of my being. It was what he had done with Shayla. I'd loved my parents dearly, but Shayla had been my other half. He'd purposely saved her death for last, and he'd made sure I'd been there to witness it.

It felt like Keelan took forever to get the car started and drive away from Ethan's house. My knee bounced with barely contained anxiety. Every minute that passed as we made our way back home felt like it was ticking by way too quickly.

When we were almost there, a warm hand smoothed over my bouncing thigh. I stilled and glanced at Creed next to me.

He was staring intently at me with a frown. I could see his questions before he thought to speak them. To prevent him from asking, I looked to Knox in the front seat. "Can you hand me my purse?"

Knox picked it up from the floor on the passenger's side and passed it back to me. I pulled out my gun that I'd had tucked into the back of my shorts under my shirt. I had hidden it there before the police and EMS had arrived to help Isabelle. I kept myself busy by flicking the safety on my pistol and putting it back inside my purse.

To my relief, the rest of the ride home was quiet. No one really said anything until we got to the guys' house to "wait for Logan." I was pretty certain it was due to their worry for Colt and the shock of what had happened to Isabelle.

As soon as we got inside, Keelan and Knox announced that they were going to search the house just in case. Creed stayed with me in the living room and took a seat on the couch. I purposely stood by the little table by the front door where the guys kept their keys in a bowl.

I had hoped Keelan would drop my keys there when he came inside. He hadn't. Instead, he'd pocketed them. After a quick freak-out, I realized that was actually a good thing. They would need my car. Very quietly, I plucked Keelan's Jeep keys out of the bowl and hid them in my fist behind my back.

Keelan and Knox returned to the living room at the same time. Keelan took a seat next to Creed on the couch, but Knox came to me. He looked me up and down in an assessing way. I felt like he was searching for lies, but he was probably just trying to see if I was all right.

I could see his intent to touch me and say something. Before he could do either, I moved around him and walked toward the twins' side of the house. "Logan should be here any minute. I'm going to wash my hands."

They didn't stop me, but I felt the weight of their eyes on me until I disappeared down the hall. I passed the bathroom and went right into Creed's room. I shut the door quietly and rushed to the window near the foot of Creed's bed. After pushing back the curtains, I tried to be quiet as I unlocked the window and pulled it open. Popping out the screen was going to make some noise, so I took a moment to pull out my personal cell and type out a text. Then I stood on Creed's bed to get level with the window before I knocked the screen off with one strong kick. I climbed out quickly.

I ran as fast as I could to Keelan's Jeep in the darn wedge heels I had chosen to wear to Ethan's party. Using the key fob, I unlocked the Jeep. Just as I ripped open the driver's door, I sent the text I had typed out and tossed my phone in the oleander bushes that separated my house from the guys'. I couldn't afford to keep it on me anymore.

I knew I had a small amount of time to pull out of the driveway before the guys came rushing out to stop me. Working fast, I started the car and shifted into reverse. I floored it out of the driveway and just as I was in the street shifting the car into drive, the Stones' front door opened. I looked away before I could see them. If I spared one glance at them, I'd hesitate, and I didn't have the time. So I floored it again. Only when I was speeding down the road did I glance in the rearview mirror. It hurt my heart to see the three of them in the street watching me drive away.

The text I had sent was to our group chat.

· · ·

Me: The Sheriff has Colt. I'm sorry I lied. I couldn't tell you the truth. Logan isn't coming. Take my car and go to my closest safe house. You know which one I'm talking about, Creed. Directions to it, keys, and cash are in my go bag in the trunk. Leave your phones behind and only use cash if you need to pay for anything. I will get Colt and we will meet you there. I love you.

2

I TOOK OFF MY WEDGES IN THE CAR AS SOON AS I PARKED IN Desert Stone Fitness's parking lot. There was only one other vehicle in the lot. It was a truck I knew belonged to the sheriff, parked near the entrance.

Because it was the middle of the night, all the lights should have been off and the doors locked. Yet I walked right through an unlocked front door into a brightly lit, empty gym. Even the music that normally played through the built-in speakers in the main room was on. With the lack of people inside, the music felt louder.

I didn't see Colt or the sheriff in the main room, so I was going to have to search for them. With my gun held out in front of me, I started with the offices behind the front desk, then I moved to the locker rooms. My heart, which had already been trying to beat its way out of my chest, boomed painfully each time I stepped into a different room.

By the locker rooms was the entrance to the indoor pool. I headed there next. Slowly, I opened the door and stepped inside. The smell of chlorine instantly filled my nose. The only lights on were the lights inside the pool, which gave the room a dim bluish hue.

The moment I saw the sheriff standing at the other end of the long, rectangular pool, the sound of the door closing behind me echoed loudly in the room. He held a gun to the back of Colt's head, who was sitting in a rolling desk chair at the very edge of the pool with his feet dangling over the water. If he tried to stand, Colt would fall right in. His ankles were bound together and his eyes were covered with thick black tape. There was a rag shoved into his mouth. His hands were behind his back, which told me they were bound as well.

Sheriff McAllister greeted me with a menacing smile, and he tracked me with his cruel eyes as I made my way closer, gun aimed at him.

"Took you long enough," he said. "I'm surprised you were the first one to get here."

My stomach dipped with fear at his implication. I was relieved I was here first, but the thought of Mr. X walking through the door at any moment made my breathing turn shaky. However, it would be better if Mr. X came here. Because if he was here, it meant he wasn't with Knox, Keelan, and Creed. It meant that they could get away to somewhere safe without being followed.

"I'm here. What now?" I replied.

The sound of my voice made Colt sit up straighter and he tried to speak around his gag.

"We wait," the sheriff said.

For Mr. X.

"Then let Colt go," I said as I stopped walking about twenty feet from him.

The sheriff pushed the barrel of his gun against the back

of Colt's head, making him lean forward. "He stays to make sure you cooperate."

My mind raced. If Colt was still here when Mr. X arrived, Mr. X would kill him. I eyed the pool and a far-fetched plan came to me. "If you push on Colt any harder, he will fall into the pool."

"Then you better be good," the sheriff said.

"But then you'd lose your leverage, and my boyfriend happens to be an amazing swimmer."

Everything in me stilled as I hoped and waited for what I said to click for Colt. It couldn't have been more than a second or two after I spoke, but it felt like an eternity until Colt lunged forward and fell into the pool.

I watched the sheriff's eyes widen before they shifted to me. I should have pulled the trigger right then. I'd had such confidence that I could do it before being faced with this decision, but my finger hesitated. No matter how evil the sheriff was, he was still a human being—a life.

That hesitation gave the sheriff time to aim his gun at me. There wasn't any hesitation in his eyes. I tried to jump out of the way. The sound of a gunshot filled and echoed in the large room. Searing pain ripped across my upper arm, making me cry out. I landed on my hands and knees on the hard floor. Ignoring the pain in my arm, I aimed my gun back in the sheriff's direction and pulled the trigger twice.

I missed him both times as he bolted through the door that led to the men's locker room.

When he was out of sight, I got to my feet and ran for the pool. Colt was at the bottom of its deepest part. Gun still in my hand, I dove into the water, spearing down toward him. I kicked as hard as I could to get to him faster. As soon as he was in reach, I pulled the rag from his mouth, wrapped my hurt arm around him, and pushed off the bottom of the pool to help propel us up. That boost only helped so far. I wasn't a strong swimmer to begin with, and with the pain in my arm and the extra weight of pulling Colt, the surface felt so far away. My lungs began to burn and panic built in me.

Just when I was about to succumb to that panic, my hand breached the surface. The instant my head was above water, I sucked in delicious air and brought Colt's head up.

He gasped for air. "Shiloh."

"I got you," I said as I swam us toward the edge of the pool, breathing loudly.

"Take your time. Don't overexert yourself," Colt instructed.

Too late. My body was already feeling weak. The only reason we were staying above water was the strength in my legs.

I got us to the edge of the pool and a small bit of relief hit me. It was short-lived, though. We didn't have time to waste.

Using the pool deck, I pulled us to the shallow end. Once Colt was able to stand in the water, I got to work helping him remove the tape around his eyes. I tried to be gentle, but he still hissed when the tape pulled on his hair.

I let out a whimper at the sight of his aquamarine eyes. He leaned forward and rested his forehead against mine. "It's okay. We're okay."

No. We aren't.

I gave him and myself three seconds to comfort each other before pulling away. "We need to get out of here."

I had to go underwater and use my teeth to rip the tape from around his ankles. The last thing bound were his wrists.

They were handcuffed. "I don't have the keys," I said in a panic.

Colt shifted in the water, moving his cuffed hands under his butt and legs until he had his hands in front of him. "This is fine for now. Let's get out of here," he said, nodding toward the closest pool ladder.

I climbed out first and turned to help him. Water fell from us and our soaked clothes, drenching the pool deck.

Colt grabbed me just above my elbow, his eyes wide as they locked on to where the sheriff had shot me. "You're hurt."

I finally looked at the wound. Blood was spilling down my arm from a long, narrow gash across my upper arm. "It's not something we can worry about right now." I grabbed one of his wrists above where he was cuffed and pulled on him as I walked quickly toward the door.

"I heard gunshots when I was in the water. Did he shoot you?" Colt asked as he kept up with me.

I let go of him to open the door into the main room of the gym. "I was stupid and hesitated pulling the trigger. I barely had time to get out of the way." I was lucky to be alive. If I hadn't jumped out of the way when I had, the shot would have killed me.

"Don't be so hard on yourself, babe. Shooting someone isn't something you should not hesitate doing."

I didn't respond to that. This wasn't the time or place to argue.

As we walked into the main room of the gym, I froze after a few steps.

"What's the matter?" Colt whispered behind me.

I brought my gun out in front of me before continuing on. "The music is off."

The front desk was where the music was controlled, and I doubted the sheriff had decided to turn it off before he left.

I let go of Colt's wrist so I could hold my gun with two hands. "Stay behind me."

He did so quietly as we walked through the gym.

"What are you guys doing here?" a voice asked when we were passing the front desk, heading for the exit.

Colt and I spun around. Gun pointed at the source, I was surprised to see that it was Derek coming up behind us. He was out of his Desert Stone uniform, dressed in jeans and a forest-green T-shirt that made the red in his hair stand out. His eyes widened and he froze next to the front desk. He put his hands up slowly. "What the hell?"

"What are you doing here?" Colt asked.

"I was driving home. I saw that all the lights were on and a truck was speeding out of the parking lot. Keelan's Jeep is out front. So I stopped by to see if everything was all right," he explained quickly.

It had probably been the sheriff speeding away in the truck. I lowered my gun. "You shouldn't have come here."

The moment I said that, someone stepped out from the hall that led to the offices behind the front desk.

My heart stopped beating. My lungs stopped working. Time even seemed to pause as my eyes drifted to the left and met coal depths that had haunted my nightmares and reality for years. He was wearing a black Desert Stone hoodie with the hood over his head. The corner of his pale mouth lifted in a terrifying smirk as he pulled a chef's knife—the same knife he had killed my family with—from the pouch pocket of the hoodie.

"No!" I screamed at the same time Colt yelled, "Derek! Watch out!"

Derek turned and ducked just as Mr. X slashed his knife at him. Mr. X went to strike Derek again, knife raised in the air. I aimed my gun for his chest and this time I didn't hesitate to pull the trigger.

The gun clicked, but didn't fire.

"Shit!" It had malfunctioned.

Derek caught Mr. X's forearm before he could bring the knife down on him. Colt stepped toward them with the intention to help Derek.

I grabbed his arm, yanking him back. His hands were cuffed, and he would only get himself killed.

Tap. Rack. Bang. Logan's voice filled my head, reminding me how to try to fix my gun. Quickly, I used my palm to tap the bottom on the magazine. Then I pulled the slide back and tilted the gun to the side. The live round that had refused to fire fell out along with a little bit of water. I made sure I pulled the slide as far back as it would go so it properly sprang a new round into place before releasing it. Praying to any deity who would listen that I'd fixed the issue, I aimed again at Mr. X.

Derek had a good amount of muscle on him, but he was struggling against Mr. X. With how close they were and how badly I was shaking, I wasn't confident in my shot. Mr. X's other hand came up and he tried to punch Derek. His many years of self-defense training seemed to kick in then and Derek blocked. He adjusted his stance to give himself better purchase. Moving swiftly, Derek twisted his body to the side and Mr. X fell forward. Derek released Mr. X's arm and punched him in the cheek. Mr. X stumbled a few feet, refusing to let himself fall to the floor.

"Derek, move!" I shouted. Mr. X's back was to me, but if I shot and he happened to move, I could hit Derek.

Derek glanced at me and saw I had my gun aimed. Mr. X turned as Derek leaped behind the front desk. I pulled the trigger just as Mr. X faced me. My gun fired and Mr. X's body jerked inward as the bullet hit his chest.

Pulling that trigger and seeing it hit him unlocked something in me. My rage surged to the surface. My rage for what he had taken from me, what he had done to me, and the threat he posed to those around me. I shot him again and again, stepping closer and closer with each bullet that left my gun.

Mr. X's shoulders jerked and his feet stumbled backward each time a bullet hit his chest. I just kept shooting and shooting. I didn't stop until he finally fell to the floor.

I stood there, frozen as I stared at Mr. X's unmoving body. Fear and disbelief wouldn't let me look away.

Was it over?

Was I free?

"Shiloh," Colt said tentatively before placing one of his cuffed hands over my good arm.

I lowered my gun and made myself look away to face Colt. As soon as our eyes met, my shoulders sagged. He lifted his arms and put them around my shoulders. I wrapped my arms tightly around his middle and buried my face in his chest.

"Are you guys all right?" Derek asked and I could hear him moving closer to us.

I didn't think I was, but I was alive, and Colt was alive. That was all I could ask for.

"We need to call the police," Colt said, avoiding answering. He lifted his arms off my shoulders and stared down at where I was hurt on my arm. "We need to do something about this. It won't stop bleeding."

"I don't have any cell service for some reason," Derek said.

I turned to see Derek heading back behind the front desk toward the landline. As he went to reach for it, a rumbling, deep, and horrifying chuckle made us all freeze.

I spun toward Mr. X in time to see him sit up slowly. His eyes were locked solely on me as he got to his feet.

How?

As if reading my mind, Mr. X lifted his Desert Stone hoodie, revealing a black bulletproof vest beneath. His eyes glinted with delight as I backed away, running into Colt. Mr. X tsked as he wagged his finger at me. "You've been a very, very bad girl, Shiloh."

His voice sent a shiver through me. I did my best to ignore it as I brought my gun up, aiming for his head this time. All he did was stand there, eyes bright, with a crazed grin. I pulled the trigger, but the gun didn't fire. The trigger had locked back. I was out of bullets.

I let out a curse. "Run," I said, grabbing Colt's arm and bolting for the door.

Derek quite literally climbed and leapt over the front desk. He was right behind us as we barreled our way out and into the parking lot.

As we ran to Keelan's Jeep and Derek to his own car, I pulled out Keelan's keys from my pocket. I pressed the unlock button on the key fob and of course, it didn't work. Diving into the pool to save Colt with the keys in my pocket had broken it. I'd have to unlock the car with the regular key.

I had the key ready in my hand as I approached the driver's door. I jammed it into the keyhole and unlocked the car as fast as I could. As soon as I was inside, I unlocked Colt's door and tossed my gun in the cup holder in the center console. I made the mistake of looking toward the gym. Walking briskly, Mr. X was heading straight for us.

"Start the car!" Colt yelled.

Shaking uncontrollably, I fumbled to get the key into the ignition, but as soon as I slid the key home, I started the Jeep. Mr. X was at my door when I shifted into reverse. Using the butt of his knife, he shattered my window. I slammed on the gas as shards of glass rained over me, cutting across my cheek, neck, arm, and thigh. The Jeep zoomed backward through the parking lot and when there was a good distance between us and Mr. X, I turned the wheel, whipping the front of the Jeep to the right. Facing the main road, I hit the brake, shifted into drive, and sped out of there.

I only glanced back for a second to make sure Derek had made it out. His car wasn't in the lot, but Mr. X stood in the center of it, eyes tracking us as we drove away.

For a while as I headed toward the interstate, all that could be heard was our heavy breathing until Colt reached for my hand closest to him, which was currently white-knuckling the steering wheel. It almost hurt to unlock my tight grip and give him my hand. Trembling profusely, I laced my fingers with his to help me stop.

Feeling it, he squeezed my hand tightly. "What's the plan?"

"Before I explain, can you get the burner phone from my purse?" I asked him as I nodded toward the backseat.

Colt twisted in his seat to reach back to grab it. He searched inside until he found the basic phone.

"Can you call your brothers on each of their phones? If

they don't answer, then we'll know they listened to me and they're headed where we're headed."

Colt dialed a number and brought the phone up to his ear. It wasn't long before he hung up. "Creed's phone went straight to voicemail."

I nodded and waited silently as he called Knox and then Keelan next. Both of their phones were turned off as well.

I let out a heavy, relief-filled sigh and relaxed against the headrest. "They're headed to my safe house in Colorado. I have a property in the mountains there."

"The other one is in Alaska, right?"

"Yeah," I said and began telling him how the night had unfolded, starting with Creed and I discovering all of my underwear at my house missing. When I got to the part where we'd found Isabelle, my voice broke. Colt grabbed my hand again and held it tightly. As I focused on the road, I blinked a bunch of times to try and stop the burning in my eyes. I held my composure as I continued, finishing with finding him and the sheriff at Desert Stone Fitness.

"I didn't feel my phone vibrating in my pocket when Creed and Knox called," Colt explained. "And when I finally did and saw I had a bunch of missed calls from them, I had a feeling something was wrong. That's why I went outside where it was quiet. So I could hear. When I was far enough away from the music playing at the party, Creed was calling me again and before I could answer…" He let go of my hand to touch the back of his head. He winced a little and brought his hand out in front of him. The tips of his fingers had blood on them.

I reached behind his head. "Let me see."

He turned a little in his seat to show me. A small spot of blond hair was red. Gently, I moved his hair out of the way so I could see how badly he was hurt. He had an inch-long cut on his scalp, near the bottom of his skull.

"I don't think you'll need stitches," I said as I stared back at the road.

"You do." He gestured to my arm where I had been shot. "Is it still bleeding?"

I didn't bother glancing at it. I could feel the blood dripping off me and to the floor between the driver's seat and the door.

I caught Colt looking me over and staring down at my lap. He said, "You're covered in glass. You should find somewhere to pull over."

"I'm too scared to pull over right now," I said honestly.

He nodded.

I got us on the interstate, heading north. We were both quiet and lost in our thoughts for at least an hour, until I needed to shift in my seat to be more comfortable. The glass shards in my lap spilled between my thighs. I read over the signs on the side of the road, looking for the nearest gas station.

As I took the next exit, I was reminded of something vital. "Shit!"

Startled by my outburst, Colt's head whipped to face me. "What?"

"Can you check to see if I have cash in my wallet, please?"

Colt took my wallet from my purse and looked through it. He pulled out two twenties.

It took a tremendous amount of restraint to calmly pull into the gas station and park in the farthest, darkest corner of the lot. Turning off the Jeep, I climbed out. Glass fell off of me and onto the ground.

We wouldn't make it to the safe house with forty dollars. It was too long of a drive. We'd run out of gas before then. I let a little bit of rage out by slamming the Jeep's door. With my hands on my hips, I moved toward the back of the car and tried to think.

I heard Colt climb out. "Hey," he said softly as he rounded the car. "Talk to me."

When he was close enough, I leaned my forehead against his chest. "We have to drive nearly eight hundred miles. We don't have enough money to make it there and we can't risk using a credit card or pulling more money from an ATM. There are cameras around everywhere. If we're traced somewhere pulling out cash..." I let out a sigh. "We can't do anything that would show what direction we are headed in. Especially now that Mr. X is working with the sheriff."

Colt started patting his pockets and reached into his front left. "He didn't take my wallet," he said as he pulled it from his pocket. "Let me see if I have cash." He opened his leather bifold and found a thin stack of ones and fives. He counted it and sighed. "I have eighteen dollars."

I stepped away from him and raked my fingers through my still-damp, tangled hair to rub my scalp. I had prepared for every scenario but this. Logan has prepared me for everything but this. "I have money in my go bag. I have money stashed under the backseat of my car. I even have a gun with an extra magazine stashed in my car. But none of that matters because I sent all of it with your brothers. I don't regret it. They needed to leave, and I needed to get you, but I have fucked us. Not only do we not have enough money to make it to the safe house, my only gun is no better than a paperweight because it's out of bullets. And if we don't make it to Colorado, your brothers will worry and will no doubt try to find us, or worse, come back here. *And* since I told them to leave their phones behind because they could be traced, we have no way of contacting them."

"What if you called Logan or Ian?" he asked.

"Logan is exactly who I would call in this situation, but he hasn't returned my calls. Which means he's probably dead. But I can't afford to think about that because I'll fall apart and we can't afford for me to fall apart," I said, my voice turning into a growl. "I don't have Ian's number on me. There's another burner phone in my go bag with two numbers on it. One of the numbers belongs to Ian. I think the other belongs to one of Logan's ex-Navy SEAL buddies. Logan said I'm not allowed to call those numbers unless he's dead and I have no other choice." I let out a humorless laugh and stared up at the night sky. I needed to calm down. Getting upset right now would only make this situation worse. With a heavy sigh, I looked back at Colt. "Logan has always been my go-between with Ian. He thought it was safer that way. Ian's only ever called me once in the past, to tell me about one of the girls Mr. X had murdered. Logan was tied up with something else at the time and they didn't want me to be blindsided if I happened to see it on the news."

Colt was quiet as he stared at me. By the pensive look he wore, I knew he was thinking. "My cousin, Micah, lives a little over an hour from here. We'd have to go out of the way, but he'll help us."

I remembered Micah. I had met him at Keelan's birthday party. "Do you really want to drag him into this?"

His eyes locked with mine and I could see that he didn't. "What choice do we have?"

3

WE WERE AT HALF A TANK OF GAS AS WE PULLED UP TO
MAD Mechanics, an auto repair and restoration shop that
Micah was one of the owners of. On the drive here, Colt had
called Micah. It had been around three in the morning when
he had called, so it had taken a few tries to get ahold of
Micah. When Micah had finally answered, Colt had tried not
to tell him much, but Micah had pressed. Colt had ended up
saying we needed help, that I was hurt, he needed a way to
get handcuffs off, and he would explain everything when we
saw Micah. After asking how badly I was hurt, Micah had
told Colt to have us meet him at his shop. As soon as Colt
had hung up the burner phone, I'd tossed it out the window
as we got back on the interstate.

As we pulled up, the first thing that stood out was that
the building was a really nice light gray with black and red
accents. The lights were on inside and Micah was standing
by an open service-bay door. He waved us over, wanting us
to pull in. As I drove up to the bay door, I noticed that
there was a motorcycle and two classic cars parked in the

lot. One of the cars was hot-rod red and the other was black.

Micah closed the bay door after we pulled in and parked. With a quick glance around, I took in the large garage. It seemed like the right half of it was designated for repairing and the left was for restoration.

Colt and I climbed out at the same time. I had put my wedges back on before heading here. They were the worst shoes to run away in, but it wasn't like I had other options to help protect my feet. The floor on the driver's side was covered in glass and it probably wasn't wise to walk around an auto shop barefoot.

Micah appeared as I remembered. He had raven hair that was shaved on the sides and had a few inches of length on the top. He was wearing a heather-gray T-shirt that tightly hugged his muscled, tattooed biceps. From what I could see, tattoos covered every inch of his arms and the tops of his hands and some of his fingers. His bottom lip was pierced with a small, matte black hoop that he was flicking with his tongue as he watched me climb out of Keelan's Jeep.

I could feel his aquamarine eyes that were identical to Colt's and Creed's roam over me, taking in my appearance. I knew I didn't look great. The glass from the window had cut me up pretty good across my cheek and neck and both had dried streaks of blood on them. My arm looked horrific. The bleeding had stopped, but what looked like a drying crimson curtain covered my arm from where I'd been shot all the way down to my elbow.

Micah held a schooled look as he did his assessment of me before his eyes shifted to Colt, who had rounded the Jeep to meet me. Micah tilted his head to the right. "Let's go into my office."

We followed him into what appeared to be the shop's front lobby, where customers would wait while their cars were being worked on. The walls were painted in light gray and behind the reception desk was a steel-paneled accent wall with the MAD Mechanics logo mounted on it. Micah led us down a hall behind and to the left of the reception desk. We passed restrooms and an employee lounge until we approached an open door. Inside, the light was on. Micah walked in first, then Colt. I was the last to go in.

Once I was inside, I saw that it was a large office with three desks. I also noticed that there were two men sitting behind two of the desks. I could only assume that they were the other two owners of MAD Mechanics. Both were silent as we entered. By their lack of surprise, I had a feeling that they had been expecting us.

Micah turned to face us and leaned against the front of what I assumed was his desk. He folded his arms across his chest. "This is Alaric and Daxton." He nodded at the other two men in the room. "Dax, Rick, this is my cousin, Colt, and his…friend, Shiloh."

Micah, Alaric, and Daxton. Their initials spelled out MAD. Micah didn't point out who was who, but I finally noticed that there were name plaques on each of their desks.

I came to stand next to Colt and took one of his cuffed hands in mine.

Micah watched as I did that and eyed the cuffs. "Want to tell me what the hell is going on?"

Colt opened his mouth to speak, but I squeezed his hand to stop him. He glanced at me questioningly.

I glanced at Dax and Rick, then back at Micah. "I'm sorry to drag you into this."

"What have you dragged us into?" Alaric asked. His voice was deep and oozed authority.

I faced him, taking in his appearance. He was wearing an Arizona Diamondbacks ball cap over what looked like short brown hair. His eyes were a slightly darker shade of brown than his hair and he was just as heavily tattooed on his arms as Micah. One tattoo in particular caught my eye. It was of a bone frog, and I could see it clearly with how he rested both his elbows on his desk, his fingers laced together in front of his mouth.

"Have you heard of the name Xander Xenos?" I asked.

"The media just gave him a nickname," Colt started to say.

"The X Killer," Daxton said. He was the least tattooed of the three and honestly seemed like the most approachable out of them. He had kind forest-green eyes and soft-looking, shoulder-length, golden-blond hair.

Micah and Alaric stared at Dax questioningly.

Daxton looked from one to the other and shrugged. "True crime and serial killers fascinate me."

Micah's eyes flicked from me to Colt. "Why are you bringing up a serial killer?"

I swallowed down my nerves and steeled myself for what I was about to tell them. "My name is Shiloh McConnell and I'm the reason why Xander Xenos is a serial killer."

Silence filled the room.

"Why do I recognize the name McConnell?" Daxton asked, frowning as he turned toward his computer and opened a web browser.

"X murdered Shiloh's family and nearly killed her, too," Colt said.

Dax's brows rose as he read over what looked like a

news article.

"You won't find me mentioned anywhere," I told him.

He glanced at me. "Why?"

"Because she's in witness protection," Colt answered for me.

I cleared my throat. "The article you're reading talks about the night my family was murdered a little over a year and a half ago, but what it doesn't say is that I was the sole survivor. Mr. X, which is how I know him, used to be my freshman English teacher. He developed an obsession with me and then stalked me for years until the night he killed my family in front of me. When I didn't feed into his fantasy he had of us being together, he tried to kill me, too. I got away and ever since that night, I've been in witness protection and he's been searching for me. Because he hasn't been able to find me, he's been raping and killing girls around my age who look like me to satisfy his obsession."

The room went quiet again.

"Let me guess," Alaric said, recovering from the shock the quickest. "He's found you."

"Yes," I answered.

Micah let out a curse and stared right at Colt. "Do Knox and Keelan know about this?"

"She's their girlfriend. Of course they know," Colt said.

Micah's eyes dropped to our hands. "Theirs?"

"Ours," Colt corrected.

Micah huffed a laugh. "I knew you and Creed shared, but I didn't think…" He trailed off, shaking his head as if astonished. "That explains why I couldn't tell which one of you was dating her at Keelan's party. All four of you acted like she was the center of your world. It was so shocking, especially seeing Knox act that way."

Him talking about Keelan's birthday party reminded me of the episode I'd had right in front of him. "What you saw at Keelan's birthday with me—when I had that moment—"

"You have PTSD," Micah said, and his eyes flicked to Alaric for only a second before they were back on me. "I'm guessing it stems from what happened to you and your family?"

I nodded.

Micah's gaze moved to Colt. "Speaking of your brothers. Where are they? Do they know you're here?"

"I have a safe house," I said. "I sent them ahead of us. Colt had been taken and—"

"Taken?" Micah and Alaric blurted at the same time.

"By the X Killer?" Daxton asked with wide eyes.

Colt sighed and calmly began telling them everything that had happened.

After Colt and I had explained everything, the uncertainty and tension that had been coming off of Micah and Daxton when Colt and I had first arrived seemed to dissipate. Alaric, however, still seemed standoffish and reluctant to help.

I caught Alaric staring at the scars around my wrists and inner arm. Then he frowned at where I had been shot and said with a curt tone, "You need stitches. Go clean up your arm in the bathroom."

I felt Colt go tense next to me. As if sensing that he was going to hulk out, Micah put a hand on Colt's shoulder and insisted that he come with him and Daxton to try to get the cuffs off his wrists.

Biting my tongue, I did as Alaric told me and went into

the women's bathroom down the hall to get cleaned up. I tried not to look at myself in the mirror. I knew I looked haggard, and I didn't have the luxury to care right now.

When I finished cleaning my arm the best I could, I returned to see that Alaric had moved a spare chair next to his desk. He nodded toward it. "Sit."

The moment I did, he dropped two pills in my hand and a bottle of water. I could tell it was just over-the-counter pain medicine.

"Thanks," I said and swallowed them down.

He didn't respond. Instead, he opened the bottom drawer of his desk and pulled out two bottles. One I recognized right away. "Pick your poison, because this is going to hurt," he grumbled as he held out a bottle of Jack and a fancy bottle of bourbon.

I didn't want to drink his nice bourbon and I knew I liked Jack, so I reached for the whiskey. I could feel him watching as I removed the cap on the bottle and took a quick swig. His brows lifted slightly before he busied himself with putting on a pair of plastic gloves like those used in a hospital or by tattoo artists. As I took another swallow of Jack, I eyed the suture supplies and bandaging he had laid out on his desk.

Colt, Micah, and Daxton returned as I brought the bottle of Jack to my lips again. I took a big drink because Alaric was about to start. I wasn't afraid of the pain. Just the anticipation of it.

Handcuff-free, Colt grabbed a chair that was sitting in front of Daxton's desk and brought it to sit in front of me. He watched as I took another drink, then a third because Alaric wheeled his chair close.

"Ready?" Alaric asked.

I nodded and Colt took my hand. As soon as I felt the

needle pierce my skin and I realized I could endure it, I took one last drink of the Jack before setting it on Alaric's desk.

Micah whistled as he watched me from where he stood behind Colt. "Not even a wince."

"Not my first time getting stitches," I said.

"Not your first time drinking Jack either, it seems," Alaric said as he tied the first stitch.

The corner of Colt's mouth lifted. "Don't ever play a drinking game with her."

I wanted to smile, but what had once been a happy memory of beating Ethan at a drinking game was now tainted. Just thinking of him reminded me of Isabelle and now wasn't the time to unbury what I felt when it came to her. Seeing my lack of reaction, Colt ran his thumb over the top of my hand.

"Did that X guy torture you?" Alaric asked.

I tensed up and Colt's hand tightened around mine.

"You have scars that show you were tied up," Alaric added, and he sewed another stitch.

Maybe it was the adrenaline mixed with the Jack that caused the truth to barrel its way out of my mouth. "He tied me by my wrists and ankles to my bed with rope and in order to get free, I twisted and pulled on that rope for hours. I tore away my skin and I didn't even feel it."

"Did you get free?" Daxton asked.

"I heard him coming down the hall just as I got one wrist free," I answered. "I had a pen on my nightstand. I grabbed it before he came into my room." Images of him dancing with my sister's dead body flashed in my head and I shook my head to make them go away. "I stabbed him through the cheek with it and got myself free."

All of them went quiet and I was relieved the questioning

seemed to be done. I glanced at Alaric and the job he was doing on my arm. He was currently laser-focused on tying his third stitch.

"Did you learn how to suture when you were a Navy SEAL?" I asked him, needing to fill the silence. Plus, he was the one who'd started with the personal questions.

His hands stilled and his eyes turned even more guarded when they flicked to mine. "What makes you think I was a SEAL?"

Micah seemed to go still behind Colt. I glanced at Daxton, who was sitting behind his desk; he also appeared to have tensed. I pointed to the same spot on my outer forearm where I'd seen his bone frog tattoo. "My uncle has a bone frog on his bicep. I know what that tattoo means because he was a SEAL for many years. How long did you serve?"

Alaric focused back on stitching me up. "Four years."

Micah and Daxton seemed to relax slightly, then both looked a little surprised when Alaric asked, "What about your uncle?"

"Eleven years," I answered.

"What does your uncle do now?" Alaric asked.

"He's a U.S. Marshal."

Alaric frowned. "Why isn't he with you now? Protecting you from this killer?"

"He trained me to protect myself so he could help capture Mr. X."

Alaric's frown deepened.

"Trained you how?" Daxton asked.

"To fight. To shoot." I met Colt's eyes. "To disappear."

"I can't imagine a little thing like you doing much damage in a fight," Micah said. "He should have stayed with you."

"She may be tiny," Colt told his cousin, "but I've seen her ground Keelan."

Micah's brows rose.

I had caught Keelan off guard that day he had snuck up on me. There was no way I could truly beat Keelan if we really sparred.

"I noticed when we were in the shop that the window on the driver's side was shattered," Daxton said. "I can put a new one in pretty quickly, if you'd like."

I looked to Colt. "Where we're headed is going to be cold."

Taking that as a yes, Daxton stood and walked out of the office.

Silence filled the room again, until Alaric asked another question. "Is that a GPS tracker around your ankle?"

Colt failed to hide the irritation on his face, but kept quiet.

I looked down at my ankle. For Ethan's party I'd had it around my wrist. I'd been worried how it would look with my heels. Appearances had stopped being important when I'd been driving to Desert Stone Fitness to rescue Colt. I had moved my tracker where it belonged around my ankle. It fit properly there and was less likely to fall off. "Yes. It's so my uncle can find me if he needs to." That was, if he was still alive.

Before my thoughts could even decide to spiral, Micah spoke. "Where is the safe house you're headed to?"

I met his eyes. "I'm sorry, but I won't tell you that."

He frowned. "You won't tell me where you're taking my family."

"Yes, they are your family, and your desire to know is understandable, but they're my family, too," I said with an even and firm voice. "I'm not saying my claim is better than yours. I am not telling you because the fewer people who know, the safer I can keep them."

"I wouldn't say anything to anyone," Micah pushed.

I didn't back down. "No."

Micah looked to his cousin.

Colt gave him a sad smile. "She said no."

Micah actually seemed surprised that Colt wouldn't tell him. Not that Colt could; he only knew that it was in Colorado.

"Don't take it personally, Micah," Alaric said as he finished tying one last stitch. "Respect the fact that she's doing everything she can to keep your cousins safe, even if it means upsetting you."

I was a little surprised he'd spoken up for me.

Micah scowled at the floor and reluctantly nodded. "Fine."

When Alaric finished, he wrapped my wound in gauze. The four of us went into the garage after that to see how Daxton was doing with replacing the Jeep's window. He informed us that it wouldn't be much longer, and we all hung out with him while he finished up.

Before we said our goodbyes, Micah pulled Colt aside. They spoke for a minute, and I saw Micah hand Colt a wad of cash. Colt put it in his pocket and the two of them hugged tightly. "Be safe," I thought I heard Micah say to him as they pulled apart from each other.

After that, Colt and I thanked Micah and his friends for their help. Then we climbed back into Keelan's Jeep and drove away.

4

WE HAD BEEN DRIVING FOR ALMOST SEVEN HOURS AND HAD just entered into Colorado. I was exhausted. The night before last, I hadn't slept well at the hotel the five of us had stayed in after finding Jacob dead on my couch, and of course, sleep hadn't happened at all last night. The more distance I put between us and Mr. X, the more the adrenaline keeping me moving seemed to wither away, and now I felt like I was running on fumes.

Colt put his hand on my thigh. "Why don't you pull over at a rest stop and let me drive for a while?"

I sat up straighter. "I'm fine."

"No, you're not," he said gently. "You've been taking charge this whole time and I've been all right with that. I understand why you've needed to be in control of things. But we're safe. X isn't here and you're exhausted. Let me take over."

Reluctantly, I pulled off the highway to a vacant rest stop and parked the Jeep.

Colt unfastened his belt. "Why don't you lay down in the back and try to sleep for a while?"

"I feel like if I relax, everything I'm trying not to think of or feel will overwhelm me and I'll fall apart," I admitted as I stared out the windshield at the mountains and trees. It was so green here compared to where we lived. The temperature outside was also colder and would continue to get colder the closer we got to the safe house. We might even see snow there. "Maybe I'm not good at burying stuff anymore or maybe it's because we're still in the thick of it. Either way, I can't help but think about and feel what's happening to us."

Colt watched me as I distracted myself with staring outside.

"Get in the backseat with me," he said, making me look at him.

"What?"

Instead of answering, he climbed out of the Jeep. I undid my belt and also got out. A cold gust of wind hit all my exposed skin, making me shiver as I opened the door to the backseat. I slid onto the bench seat in the back just after Colt did.

"What are we doing?" I asked as I turned my body toward him.

He cupped my cheek. "I'm going to help you fall asleep." He leaned in to kiss me.

The moment his lips molded to mine, I understood what he meant. I pulled back, gaping. "Here?"

His hand moved from my cheek to cup the back of my neck, holding me in place. "There's no one around to see." He pressed his lips to mine, softly. "Just focus on me." He kissed me again. This time with a little more passion.

"You're distracting me with sex?" I asked against his

lips. I'd expect this type of assertiveness from Creed, but not Colt. Well, unless Colt's Hulk side had surfaced. When that happened, he touched me and took my body as if he owned it. But he wasn't in one of his Hulk moods. Maybe it was the circumstances we were in.

Colt moved his mouth to my neck. "Sex with me better be distracting." He lightly bit me, forcing my breath to hitch and my body to arch toward him. "If I don't have your full attention when I'm fucking you, then I'm not doing it right."

Dirty Stone boy.

I should have been able to smile at that moment. Instead, I found myself blinking away the burn that instantly flared behind my eyes. As soon as I had control of myself, I asked, "Is that the plan? You're going to exhaust me with sex to help me fall right to sleep?"

He pulled back to face me. Adoringly, he tucked my hair behind my ear. "How should I do it?" He kissed my lips again. "Shall I take you hard or slow?"

He'd evaded answering because what I'd said was true. I put my hand on his chest, stopping him. "If you make love to me right now, I might start crying."

A pensive frown took over his face as his eyes searched mine. "Why is that?"

Because I don't deserve you.

And you don't deserve what I brought upon you and your brothers.

And it's taking everything I have to hold the guilt of that back from crushing me.

How did I tell someone I loved that their love made my guilt too much to bear?

I hadn't lied in the voicemail I'd left Logan. I was a piece of shit. I shouldn't have even been in this backseat with Colt, but to not be near him, to not accept his touch, especially after almost losing him, would be like denying myself air. It seemed I was damned either way. All I could do right now was choose how badly I wanted to suffer.

I couldn't tell him any of that, though. So I said, "Ask me tomorrow."

Something showed in his eyes, and I had that gut-dropping feeling he knew. Every thought that had passed through me, the struggle I was desperately trying not to let him see, he knew, and I braced myself for his reply to the point my whole body stiffened.

His fingers tightened just a little at the back of my neck. "Tomorrow." His voice was even and firm. He only said one word, yet it was enough to give me a sense of foreboding. He'd give me until tomorrow, but he wasn't happy about it, which cemented the fact that he knew.

"Lay down, Shiloh," he ordered as he grabbed the back of my knee with his other hand.

Shiloh? Looked like I'd brought out his Hulk side. Goosebumps pebbled my skin as I lay on my back across the bench seat.

Colt adjusted so that he was kneeling between my thighs. His hands slid down my bare legs until he reached my heels. He pulled them off of my feet and let them drop to the floor. Butterflies fluttered low in my belly as he unbuttoned my shorts and hooked his fingers into the top of them and my underwear. "Lift." His tone was sharp.

Doing as I was told, I pushed my hips up for him to undress me from the waist down. He dropped my shorts and underwear next to my shoes. His eyes held mine as his hands gripped me by the backs of my thighs. I sucked in a breath as he spread me open. I watched, holding my breath as his eyes dropped between my legs.

"I'm pissed," he said before his head delved between my legs.

My back arched as his hot mouth covered me and his tongue licked me from core to clit. "I know," I whimpered.

He pulled away slightly, until all I could feel was his warm breath fanning over my most private parts. "I feel like punishing you, but I know you'd just take it, thinking it's what you deserve."

His tongue began exploring me, purposely avoiding the spot he knew would get me off. Maybe he had decided to punish me.

"Tomorrow, Colt," I reminded him.

His hands on my thighs tightened before he moved his mouth to my clit.

Without thought, my hands dove for his head and my fingers fisted his hair as he attacked that spot on me, sucking, flicking, and stroking in a way that was making me lose my mind. Moans and whines ripped their way past my lips as my body writhed. I could feel my release getting closer. Desperate to get there faster, I rocked my hips against his mouth. "Colt," I begged.

His way of giving me what I wanted, one of his hands let go of my thigh and he pushed two fingers inside me. All he had to do was pump those fingers in me twice and I threw my head back, crying out. My body went simultaneously tight and loose as my climax rippled through me.

Colt didn't let up on worshiping my clit and his fingers continued stroking in and out of me, drawing out my release. Even when it did eventually fade, Colt still didn't stop.

"Colt?" I panted. It was apparent he wanted to make me come again, but everything felt more sensitive down there. What he was doing was almost too much. I was shaking all over. Every breath I took was a loud pant. I could feel my orgasm building again. Only this time, it felt different. The pleasure was more intense, almost painful, and familiar. "Colt!" I cried as my thighs squeezed around him. "You're—you!" I tried to get out between loud moans. "I'm—ah!—Colt!"

I knew what was coming. I had only experienced it once with Keelan and I couldn't get the words out to tell him. I couldn't hear it, but I knew I was screaming as my entire body curled toward Colt's head between my legs. When I came again, I collapsed back against the seat. Like the time Keelan and I'd had sex on the chair in their dining room, I felt the gush between my legs.

Colt went still.

I quickly let go of his hair and covered my face.

When he pulled his fingers from me, I peeked at him from between mine.

He was staring at me, smirking like he was proud. "That was unexpected." I watched as he brought his wet hand up to his mouth and ran his tongue along the back of it. "You taste so sweet."

I didn't have time to figure out if I enjoyed his reaction or if I was even more mortified, because he grabbed me by my hips and flipped me over onto my hands and knees. "Colt?" My whole body felt like weak spaghetti, and I wasn't sure I could come again.

"We're not done, Shiloh," he said, and I heard the sound of his zipper.

"Stop calling me that," I snapped. Yes, it was my name, but I didn't like him saying it out of anger.

He put a hand on my lower back as he brushed the head of his cock along my soaked slit. "I'll stop calling you that when you stop punishing yourself over shit you have no control over."

He cut off any reply I might have had by pushing all the way inside of me. Gasping, I threw out my hand in front of me onto the door to keep myself from falling forward. My thighs and arms trembled as they strained to keep me up. "I—"

I was cut off again as he withdrew and thrust back into me.

"I can't hold myself up," I whimpered.

He grabbed me by my hips. "Put your head down." His voice had gentled. "I got you."

I did as he said and lowered the top half of my body down on the seat. I still kept my hand against the door just in case. When he withdrew and speared back into me, his grip on my hips kept me from moving too much. I felt him pause as if to see if I was all right. After determining that I was, he seemed to unleash himself.

As he pounded into me, making me go cross-eyed with the pleasure overload, I moaned loud and long into the seat. "I don't think I can come again." I most definitely could. My real worry was if I could survive it.

"Yes, you can." He sounded so sure.

"You're going to break me."

He let out a breathy chuckle. "I could never bring myself to break any part of you." He slowed his thrusts and moved one of his hands to my shoulder. He pulled on me to sit up until my back was to his chest. I laid my head back against his shoulder, feeling too weak to hold it up. He still moved inside me, only his thrusts were slower, making me savor every sinful inch of him. His hands slid to the front of my body. One found its way up inside my shirt and under my bra. The warmth from his palm as it kneaded my breast made me close my eyes. His other hand slowly dropped south and the moment his fingers found my clit, I groaned. I threw an arm behind me to grab the back of his neck, needing to hold onto him as he began rubbing slow circles over that super sensitive spot.

Panting, my chest heaved as he pushed me toward the edge of release. Feeling me getting close, his thrusts picked up speed. I screamed as he not only sent me over the cliff, he threw me, and the fall wrecked me. I lurched forward and caught myself on my hands.

Colt's hands went back to my hips. I knew he was moments from coming when his grip tightened. To my surprise, he let me go and pulled out of me quickly. I spun around to see him stroking himself as jets of cum spilled out of him right onto the wet spot I'd created on the seat.

For a moment we just sat there trying to catch our breath.

"Why?" I said between breaths.

His eyes met mine. "Because you're not on birth control."

And just like that, reality came back to me. It had been days since I'd last taken my birth control because it and my nightmare medication had gone missing. No doubt Mr. X had taken it.

Weakly, I reached for my shorts and underwear. "I'm sorry I forgot."

Colt tucked himself back into his pants. "I didn't remember, either, until I was about to come." After he finished buttoning his pants, he frowned down at the mess we'd made on the seat.

"Now we're both going to get into trouble for coming all over Keelan's backseat," I said as I pulled my underwear and shorts on.

Colt gave me a proud smirk again. "I highly doubt you'll get in trouble for soaking the backseat. Keelan is just going to be peeved that he wasn't the one to make you do it."

An intense blush bloomed in my cheeks.

"I, on the other hand, am screwed if I don't clean this up," he said as he peeked over the backseat into the trunk. Seeing something, he reached back there and grabbed what looked like one of Keelan's gym bags. Dropping it in his lap, he unzipped it and searched inside the bag. "Perfect." He pulled out a towel and a shirt. He used the shirt to clean up the seat the best he could before laying the towel over the wet spot. When he was done, he shoved the shirt back into the bag and tossed it back in the trunk.

My eyes felt heavy, and my body completely spent.

Colt eyed me before holding his hand out to me. "Come here."

"Are you still mad at me?" I asked him tiredly.

"Yes, but I still want to hold you."

Wanting that, too, I took his hand and let him help me over to him. He leaned against the door on his side so I could lie against his chest. If he was uncomfortable, he didn't say anything. Instead, he wrapped his arms around me tightly.

It wasn't long before my heavy eyes won the battle and closed. "I'm going to have a nightmare," I whispered.

He kissed the top of my head. "I'll be here to wake you."

5

"SHILOH," A FEMININE VOICE WHISPERED.

My eyes shot open, finding myself surrounded by darkness. It was so dark I couldn't tell what was up or down, but I could feel a presence coming toward me. Everything in me told me I had to get away—to run. So I did. I ran not knowing where I was going or if I would slam into something. What I did know was that the presence I felt began chasing me. The threat I could sense from them made the hairs on the back of my neck stand up.

I blinked, or at least I thought I did, and a light appeared in the distance. As I ran for it, I could see that the light was coming from a cracked door. I blinked again and I was suddenly standing right in front of it.

The moment I saw the bloody handprint on the door, I knew where it led.

"Shiloh," the feminine voice whispered again, and that time I realized who the voice belonged to.

"Isabelle?" I said as I pushed open the door.

I braced myself to find her bleeding on the floor. The

door swung inward slowly, revealing an empty bathroom. There wasn't even a drop of blood anywhere. I walked inside the bright room toward the sink, my gaze taking in the mirror as I did. It was clean. Mr. X's message was gone and all I could see was my reflection.

Through the mirror I noticed movement over my shoulder. As if stepping out of a black abyss, Keelan appeared in the doorway behind me.

"Are you all right?" he asked me.

I opened my mouth to answer just as an alabaster face with coal eyes slid out of that black abyss behind Keelan. Before I could do or say anything, Keelan's body jerked, arching backward, his eyes going wide.

"No!" I screamed as I spun around. I reached for Keelan to pull him away from Mr. X. Before I could, Mr. X's hand wrapped around Keelan's throat, and he pulled him backward into the darkness.

Nothing mattered but the desperate need to save Keelan. Not even my fear. I went to run back into that darkness, but something caught me by my ankle. I fell forward. My hands and knees slammed down on the tile that was now covered in blood. As I tried to get up, I slipped and slid in the blood.

"Shiloh," the feminine voice called to me again and something tightened around my ankle. I glanced backward, finding Isabelle lying on the ground. She was just as I had found her at Ethan's birthday. Stabbed, bleeding, and deathly pale. Her teal hair was soaking up the blood spreading around us. Her blue eyes were wide and fixed on me. "Help me," she begged.

The sound of Keelan screaming out in pain echoed in the darkness, drawing my attention out the bathroom door.

Faced with a decision I wished I didn't have to make,

tears rolled down my cheeks as I glanced back at Isabelle. "I'm sorry." I tried to yank my ankle free.

Isabelle tightened her grip. "Please don't leave me."

A sob barreled out of me. "I'm sorry!" I yanked away again, this time getting free. Pushing to my feet, I dove into the darkness, leaving my friend to die.

∼

I woke, leaping to sit up. I barely had time to register that I was in the back of Keelan's Jeep when a hand touched my arm.

"You're safe."

Startled, I scooted away until I slammed my shoulder, then my back into one of the doors in the backseat. I looked up front and saw Colt was driving. His arm reached back toward me. He glanced over his shoulder at me for only a second before staring back at the road.

"You're safe," he repeated. "It was just a dream." He put on the car's blinker and merged to the right.

Reality came back to me and then my nightmare replayed in my head. Instantly, my stomach twisted.

I left her.

"Pull over," I begged.

"I am," Colt said.

Before Colt could bring the Jeep to a full stop on the side of the road, I had the door open, and I jumped out. I made it just a few feet before I bent over and vomited. I heaved until I had nothing left in my stomach and then heaved some more.

Hands collected my hair and held it back. "Focus on breathing. In through your nose, out through your mouth,"

Colt said as he put his hand on my lower back and began rubbing in small circles.

I did as he instructed and when it seemed like I wasn't going to heave again, I stepped away from him. He let go of my hair so he wouldn't pull it as I kept putting more space between us.

"Shiloh," he said, anger seeping into his voice.

I could feel him following me, so I stopped walking. I rubbed my eyes, hoping to ease the need to cry, before moving my hands up into my hair. "I can't have you comforting me right now, Colt."

"Why?" he asked, sounding as if he was right behind me.

I turned to face him. "Because I am barely holding it together."

He reached out to touch me. Before he could, I caught him by his wrist, stopping him. "It is taking everything I have not to fall into your arms and break," I said. "But to do that would be selfish. I love you too much to do that to you —to your brothers."

"You're not in this alone."

I let go of his wrist. "I'm well aware of that."

His expression hardened into a frown. "You almost sound like you wish you were."

My hands fisted at my sides. "This is all new for you. The fear. The uprooted life. The running and hiding. But as time passes, you will get tired of always looking over your shoulder, and when that happens, you will resent me."

He inhaled deeply, his nostrils flaring. It was clear that I'd upset him, but as he exhaled slowly, some of the tension in his body seemed to ease. "Damn it, babe." He looked away from me, staring off at the mountains behind me.

It was then that I felt how cold it was outside. Feeling the need to shiver, I moved to fold my arms over my chest.

That drew his gaze back to me. He took me in and sighed. "Let's get back in the car. It's freezing out here."

"Can I drive?" I asked, needing the distraction.

He nodded and we climbed back into the Jeep. As I pulled back onto the interstate, it took me a minute to realize where we were—less than an hour away from the safe house.

Silence filled up the car and as the minutes ticked by, that silence became more and more heavily apparent.

"You're wrong, you know," Colt said, dispelling the heaviness around us.

"About what?" I peeked at him for a second before returning my attention to the road. He was staring out his window.

"I want you to put yourself in our shoes for a moment," he said. "If my brothers and I were the ones in WITSEC and we had to run, would you run with us? Would you uproot your life?"

"I shouldn't have said any of that," I said, trying to deflect.

"It's how you feel. So answer the question." His firm voice told me that there was no avoiding this.

"Yes, I would run with you," I said.

"Do you think you would come to resent us?"

"No," I answered without thought, because I didn't need to think about it. I just knew on every level, from my head to my heart to my soul. I just knew. I didn't care what came our way or what we had to endure; as long as we were together, that was enough for me. They were enough.

I saw his point and it was a little reassuring, but my guilt was still too crushing. "You and your brothers are stronger than me. If you had been in my place, I don't think you would have even allowed yourself to get close to me to begin with."

Colt didn't deny it. Not that I expected him to. The fact that he didn't just cemented why I was a piece of shit. Realizing that unleashed Logan's voice in my head.

"You know better, Shi. What the fuck were you thinking dragging them into all of this?"

"You're being stupid, Shiloh. So unbelievably stupid. You have fucked everything up by telling them."

"I did not intend to fall in love with you or to drag you into this." My throat became tight and my resolve to stay strong wavered a little.

Colt let out a sigh. Out of the corner of my eye, I saw him look away from his window to stare at me. "I don't know for sure what I would have done if our roles were reversed. What I do know is that from the moment I first saw you, I couldn't stop thinking about you. I had to know you, and the more time I spent with you, the more I was determined to keep you."

I bit my lip so it wouldn't tremble.

"If that isn't enough to reassure you," he continued, "then look back on how you and Knox came to be. He tried to not allow himself to be with you and yet, you two are together."

One tear escaped my left eye and rolled down my cheek. I wiped it away before it could drip off my chin.

Colt put his hand on my knee. "Please stop punishing yourself because you think you've damned us by loving us. You have a bad habit of doing that."

I opened my mouth to argue, but Colt stopped me with a light squeeze of his hand. "I understand why you feel guilty. I would, too, but I want you to listen when I tell you that I wouldn't choose to be anywhere but here, with you, right now. I know it's the same for my brothers. If we need to keep reminding you of that until it sticks, then so be it."

Another tear rolled down my cheek, this time from my right eye. Colt's hand left my knee and he wiped the tear away with his thumb.

"That's not really fair for you to have to do that," I said.

"If it was over trivial things, I could see how it wouldn't be," he said. "But what you're feeling right now and what is happening is anything but. And I know it's not just the guilt you feel about us that's bothering you."

He was hinting at Isabelle.

"I wish I could take on your guilt and fight it for you." His thumb brushed across my cheek again. Not to wipe away a tear, but in a way that was loving.

I wouldn't wish what I was feeling right now on anyone.

"Is this it?" Colt asked as we pulled up to an iron gate that blocked a narrow, winding road.

"This is it," I said as I got out of the Jeep. I walked up to the side of the gate where there was a little black box nailed to a post. I opened the box, revealing a keypad. After I entered in the seven-digit code, the gate beeped and began to slide open.

I climbed back into the Jeep and drove through. About halfway to the house, the road changed from asphalt to dirt.

I caught Colt staring out the window, taking in the forest all around us. "It's really isolated," he commented.

"I think the nearest neighbor is fifteen acres to the west," I said.

He glanced at me. "You think?"

"I've only been here once, right before I moved to Arizona," I explained. "When I decided to rejoin civilization and restart my life, Logan insisted that I have another location to run to besides Alaska. It's not only farther to get to Alaska, but I also told everyone in Arizona that I was from there. The safe house I have there is even more isolated than this and would be difficult to find, but not impossible if Mr. X came searching."

"Why did you even tell anyone that you were from Alaska to begin with?" he asked.

"Because I'm a terrible liar and lies are easier to keep track of if there's some truth to them."

He nodded his understanding and returned to staring out the window just in time for the cabin to come into view. I saw my 4Runner parked outside the one-story log cabin. I exhaled audibly, feeling relieved.

"I'm relieved to see they're here, too," Colt said.

I parked Keelan's Jeep next to my 4Runner and the moment I shut off the car, the front door of the cabin opened. Knox stepped out onto the front porch, then Keelan and Creed.

As Colt and I climbed out, they looked from me to Colt and relief washed over each of them. Creed and Keelan rushed off the porch for us. Creed beelined for Colt. I watched him pass and it almost seemed as though he was refusing to look at me. Just as I began to feel unsettled by that, Keelan threw his arms around me, enveloping me with warmth. It was freezing here, and I was certain it would snow either tonight or tomorrow.

Keelan squeezed me tightly. "You scared the shit out of us."

I barely had time to hug him back before he pulled away just enough to face me. His eyes bounced all over my face and neck. He cupped my cheek and ran his hand over the scratch there. He looked like he was about to question me about it when a hand grabbed me by my elbow just below where my arm was bandaged.

I looked to see who it was and found Knox standing next to us, frowning at where I had been shot.

"What happened?" he asked as his eyes traveled to the cuts on my neck and cheek.

Keelan released me, taking his warmth with him.

I turned my body toward Knox. "I'm fine."

Colt and Creed joined us then. "She was shot," Colt said.

"What?" Keelan gaped as Knox's hand tightened around my elbow.

"I'm fine," I repeated and pulled my arm from Knox's grasp. He let go of me the moment I tried to pull away. Beginning to shiver, I folded my arms over my chest. "Why don't we go in—"

"Stop fucking lying to us, Shi," Creed snapped. The anger in his voice startled me.

I whirled to face his clearly unhappy stare. "I'm not lying. I'm okay." My words just seemed to piss him off more. "You're angry with me?"

"You left us, Shi," he said. His voice wasn't loud, but his tone was harsh and strained, as if it was taking everything in him to not combust. "You lied, played us for fools, and then took off. Do you have any idea how hard it was to leave you and come here? To trust that you'd be able to do as you said? We didn't know where you were, if you were okay..."

54

The more he spoke, the more upset he got. He kept clenching and unclenching his fists at his sides. "You promised, Shi. Run or fight, as long as we're together. You fucking promised me."

"Creed," Colt said, taking my hand in his. "She had to. She—"

I cut him off by pulling my hand away. "You're right, I broke my promise." My voice sounded numb—vacant. "Be mad at me, Creed. Fucking hate me. I hurt you. I scared you. I'm sorry for that and so much more." The numbness in my voice spread to the rest of me until I wasn't feeling cold anymore. "But I'm not sorry for what I had to do to save your brother. There wasn't any time and I had to make a tough call very quickly that made sure we all ended up safe."

"Bullshit!" Creed snarled. "You sent us away because it was easier. That's the type of shit your uncle would pull."

I looked down. Did he really believe that? And was he right?

"Creed!" Colt snapped.

Maybe I should have argued—fought to explain, but I just…I had nothing left in me to give. There was still so much to do, and my energy was in the negative. All I could do for them and for me was finish making sure we were secure and safe. When that was done, I'd fight for Creed to forgive me. Without saying another word, I slid between Knox and Keelan and headed for the house.

"What the fuck are you doing?" I heard Colt snap behind me. "Do you really believe she would have done what she did if she had any other choice? Why the fuck are you so quick to pass judgment without hearing her side?"

"Why didn't she have a choice?" Knox asked as I opened the door to the cabin.

"Because the sheriff told her he'd kill me if she didn't come alone," Colt said.

I didn't hear anymore once I walked inside. The wood floor creaked under my wedges as I moved through the open living space that consisted of a kitchen to the left and a small living room facing a large stone fireplace on the right. There wasn't a dining space. Just four stools that surrounded the kitchen island. A lot of the furniture was basic, a little dated, and had come with the place when Logan had bought it for me. And when I said "bought it for me," I meant that he'd been in charge of buying it with my family's money. Not the life-insurance money. The money I didn't like to acknowledge existed.

When Logan had insisted on buying another safe house and asked if he could use my family's money to do so, I hadn't wanted any part in it. I had told him he could spend all the money he wanted for all I cared. He had just rolled his eyes at me and found and bought this place. We had spent a whole three days here before I'd started my life in Arizona. I'd hoped I would never have to come here. Which was why I hadn't bothered to add any personal touches to the place. I had, however, brought and left a good chunk of my winter clothes from Alaska.

Apart from its somewhat dated furniture, it was a nice cabin. Along the far wall of the living room were two doors. One led to a bedroom and the other led to a bathroom. Farther down the far wall, past the living room, was a small hall with two more doors leading to two more bedrooms.

I headed for the hall and entered the door all the way at the end. It was the owner's suite—my room. It just had a queen bed with gray and tan plaid bedding, a nightstand with a lamp on top, a dresser, and a trunk at the end of the bed.

There was another large stone fireplace that took up the far corner of the room. A few feet in and to the left was the en suite. I headed there.

The bathroom was small. Right when you walked in, there was the sink. Next to it was the toilet and next to that was the shower. I opened up the mirror cabinet above the sink, finding a brand-new toothbrush and toothpaste. All I'd been able to do since I'd thrown up was rinse my mouth out with water at a gas station. I got to work brushing my teeth.

After I was done, I splashed water on my face in an attempt to wake myself up. I would've preferred a shower. I could still smell chlorine on my skin. Sadly, there weren't many daylight hours left to waste.

I went back into my room, took off my wedges, and went to the dresser. I pulled out a pair of jeans, a thick cream sweater, and thick socks. Pretty much everything I would need was already here for me, apart from food. There wasn't anything for the guys. I was sure they hadn't packed winter clothes in their backpacks.

I placed the clothes I'd pulled out of the dresser on the bed. Just as I removed my shirt, Knox appeared in the doorway. His eyes dropped to my green, black, and yellow Loki bra. He didn't say anything and neither did I as he watched me unbutton my shorts. His eyes followed my hands as I pushed the shorts past my hips and down my thighs until I let them drop to the floor around my feet.

There was heat in his stare. That heat warmed up my cold skin, but it wasn't enough to warm me anywhere else. There was too much going on—too much that had happened. Time felt like it was moving too quickly, and I was racing against it.

As I reached for my jeans, I felt Knox move into the

room. Jeans in hand, I faced him.

He came close enough to touch. "You're not all right." The way he said that almost felt like a question.

I debated my response, debated lying. The last thing I wanted was for him to worry. Having already lied to him many times in the past twenty-four hours, I decided against it. "No. I'm not."

His hand cupped the back of my head. "What do you need?"

"To keep moving."

His fingers snaked through my messy hair and began massaging the base of my skull. "That's avoiding."

I knew that, and I knew if I did it long enough, avoiding would become the easier choice. My eyes closed on their own and my head leaned back into his hand. "It's necessary."

"Why?" Knox's voice sounded deeper.

I opened my eyes, finding Knox leaning over me, his mouth hovering inches above mine. A few days ago, I would have closed the distance between us.

I brought my hand up and cupped his cheek. "Because it's not safe yet."

Knox pulled back a little, his eyes searching mine. "We're as safe as we can be."

"Give me until tomorrow, please?" I pleaded in a low voice. It was what I had requested of Colt even though he hadn't completely listened. Tomorrow was my finish line, what I had to get to. Until that time, I'd get everything done we needed to be safe, secure, and prepared here.

I didn't know what Knox read in my eyes, but he relented with a small nod before leaning down, bringing his mouth to mine.

His kiss was gentle at first, as if he intended it to be short. That quickly changed. He moved closer, his other hand sliding over my skin to my lower back. The way his lips caressed mine went from gentle to demanding. I should resist, yet it would be so easy to give in. Who wouldn't want to feel something good when the world was falling apart?

I put my hand on Knox's chest and pushed against him gently. Knox stilled before pulling away with a question in his eyes.

"I'm not stopping because I don't want to kiss you," I told him.

"You don't have to explain."

"It's not that I have to, Knox. I'm extending the same courtesy to you that I'd want in return. It's easy to misread something and I don't ever want you to feel like I don't want you."

Through his touch I felt him go tense. "I never wanted you to feel that way."

I sighed and rested my forehead on his chest. "I know, and I didn't say that to hurt you."

Knox's fingers continued to knead the back of my neck. "So why did you pull away?"

"There's a lot that needs to be done and there aren't a lot of daylight hours left," I said into his chest.

"Like what?"

I pulled away and out of his arms. "We don't have any food here." I got dressed as I spoke. "It's only going to get colder. It's going to snow and if it snows too much, there's a risk we could get snowed in. You and your brothers don't have proper clothing, either. So I'm going to need your sizes before I head to town."

"Or we could go with you," he suggested.

I thought about it. "A few of you can come. Either only one of the twins can come or both need to stay behind. Twins are too noticeable and rememberable. If Keelan's coming, he'll need to wear something to cover up his tattoos. There's some of Logan's clothes here. Him and Keelan are about the same size."

"Creed and I will go with you," he decided.

After getting on my shirt, I went to the trunk at the foot of the bed and pulled out a pair of boots and a bark-colored knitted beanie. I closed the trunk and sat on top of it to put on my socks and boots. "Are you sure Creed will even want to be around me?"

"I'm not going to get in the middle of you and Creed." He stuffed his hands in his pockets. "I will say that when you took off after sending us that vague text, Keelan had to restrain Creed to stop him from driving off and searching for you."

I looked down at the floor. "If I had any other choice, I wouldn't have left you three like that."

"We know that now."

I supposed Colt had told them everything.

"I also believed you wouldn't have left like that unless you had to. It was obvious something was going on when we left Ethan's. You were on edge and distracted." Knox moved to stand in front of me. He grabbed my chin and made me look up at him. "It wasn't easy having faith that you and Colt would meet us here. You were going into a dangerous situation and leaving felt like we were abandoning you two."

"I can see why that was hard," I said. "Thank you for leaving despite it."

As Knox stared down at me, his normal serious face gentled a little. "Thank you for saving my brother."

6

We headed out after retrieving money and my Colorado driver's license, which had my picture but a different alias on it, from my go bag, which was the duffel bag I'd grabbed from the safe in my panic room back in Arizona. The hour drive to town was quiet for the most part. Creed rode in the backseat, frowning as he stared out the window. There were a few times when I peeked back at him through the rearview mirror as I drove us and caught him staring at me, but when he realized, he would look away. Knox sat up front with me and appeared to be sleeping. I was pretty sure he had been up since yesterday like the rest of us.

It wasn't until we were pulling up to our first stop that I broke the silence. "There will be cameras everywhere. Try to keep your head down as much as you can."

Knox opened his eyes and looked at me as if he hadn't been sleeping at all, merely resting with his eyes closed. Putting my attention back on the road, I felt rather than saw him reach out before brushing the side of my neck. "You have hair hanging out."

I brought my hand up to where he touched and felt the strand of hair he spoke of. Using one hand, I tucked it into my beanie. I'd put it on before leaving, hoping to hide my red hair. I'd need to pick up hair dye while we were out. The red was too noticeable.

Our first stop was a large, common department store. As soon as we entered, I suggested that we split up to get things done faster.

"Creed can go with you," Knox said and walked away toward the men's clothing department.

It was obvious what Knox was doing. I glanced at Creed and saw him frowning at his brother, who was walking farther and farther away.

As if feeling me watching, Creed's gaze slid to me. His frown lessened just a smidge and he sighed. "Let's go."

It seemed that Knox's plan was going to be for naught. I should have felt more upset and dwelled on the fact that Creed was mad at me. In normal circumstances, I probably would have. Maybe I was burying it with everything else because I was exhausted. Or maybe I just didn't care because I knew I was justified in doing what I'd done and that really meant I was like my uncle. No. It had to be the first. I'd make things right tomorrow.

Creed let me take the lead. I grabbed a cart and decided to start in the toiletry department. I moved quickly through the aisles, pulling things off the shelves for the guys and for me without fully stopping. Because the drive here had been silent, I'd made mental lists of things we would need.

They didn't have a huge selection of hair dye. I glanced over the small variety quickly, seeing that I had the option to go brown, which was my actual hair color. That didn't seem like a good idea. I didn't want to be more recognizable to Mr. X.

They were out of black dye. My only other option was to go with a light color. I'd have to bleach the red out of my hair. I knew the basics of how to do that, but having my phone to look up exactly how to do everything would have been really nice right now.

Cheese and rice! Knowing my luck, my hair was going to come out orange or completely ruined. Reluctantly, I grabbed a bleach hair kit and tossed it in the cart.

The next aisle was the feminine hygiene aisle, and I froze. My period had been due yesterday. The moment the crazy, panicked thought of possibly being pregnant entered my head, my rational side took over. I was on birth control. Or I had been up until a few days ago. I had a history of being a few days late when under a lot of stress. Besides, I was already getting the chocolate cravings that I always got right before and would continue to have after I started. As soon as I was able to calm down, my body would do what it was supposed to. For now, I needed to get supplies for when my period did eventually begin.

I caught Creed staring at me with a frown as I pulled the products I'd need from the shelf. I didn't have it in me to feel embarrassed. Not that I had any reason to be. He didn't say anything, so neither did I.

Farther down the aisle were condoms. Those were a must now that I was no longer taking birth control. Colt and I had already had unprotected sex. He may have pulled out, but we would not be having sex like that again.

I looked over the brands and styles of condoms that were available. I had bought condoms before, but they didn't have that kind here. I bit my lip, trying to decide which one to get.

Creed sighed. "These ones, Shi." He grabbed a few boxes off the shelf and tossed them into the cart.

"Thanks," I muttered and continued on to the next aisle.

He went back to quietly following me. Or at least until I stopped to grab something. I felt him come up behind me before his arms wrapped around my stomach.

"Shi." His arms around me tightened, molding my back to his chest. He rested his forehead on my shoulder. "I was scared, pissed off, and I'm exhausted. I said things I didn't mean because I thought..." His arms squeezed around me even more. "It doesn't matter what I thought. I was a jerk and I'm sorry."

"If you squeeze me any tighter, I'm going to pop."

Creed's arms instantly loosened, and his hands went to my hips to spin me around to face him. His mouth latched to mine and before I could process that, he pulled away just a breath. "I don't think you're like your uncle. I was lashing out." He kissed me again. It was quick, but I was prepared for it enough to kiss him back. His hands moved to cup my face and he pressed his forehead to mine. "I'm sorry."

I wrapped my arms around his waist. "It's all right, Creed."

He squeezed his eyes shut. "I felt like I was going out of my mind."

The pain I heard in his voice hurt my heart. I put my head on his shoulder and hugged him as tightly as he had hugged me. "I know. I'm sorry."

We stood there holding each other for a while. At first, I felt completely, helplessly gutted that he felt that way. I wished I could fix it. I was desperate for him to never feel that way again. That desperation quickly turned into anger, because the only way to obtain what I wanted was if Mr. X was dead.

The sun was setting by the time we returned to the cabin. Keelan and Colt came out to help unload the car. After everything was put away, Knox offered to cook something for us, and I went to go take a fast shower. The warm water from the shower relaxed me to the point I felt bone tired. I struggled to get clothes on and had to sit down on my bed after. *Just until dinner is ready,* I told myself as I lay back across the foot of the bed.

Sleep pulled me away without me even realizing it and the next thing I knew, I was being lifted. I tried to open my heavy eyes, but all I could manage to do was groan.

"It's just me, baby girl," Keelan said as he laid me somewhere else in the bed.

When I felt blankets come over me and his warm body cuddle me from behind, I drifted back to sleep.

My eyes shot open as the blankets were slowly pulled down my body. At first, all I could do was watch the shadows as they danced on the ceiling. I felt paralyzed, unable to move, unable to blink as the rest of the blankets were pulled off of me completely.

It took me a moment to realize I was home in my bed in Arizona.

Cold air kissed my exposed skin just before fingers touched the top of my foot. My heart began to beat faster when those fingers started to move up the top of my leg. I could hear heavy footsteps on the rug as someone walked along the side of the bed.

Once they reached the hem of my pajama shorts, the fingers didn't stop. They continued up my thigh, over my P.Js, over my hip and stomach, until they reached my breast. There the fingers circled around my nipple through my thin pajama top, making it harden.

The feeling of the bed dipping and their bulky body settling in the bed next to me was familiar. My body moved on its own, snuggling closer to the person who I had thought had been Knox. That had been before. Too tired, I hadn't opened my eyes before. They were wide open now. I was still unable to blink and this time I could see that it was not Knox who was in bed with me.

"Shiii...loooh," he whispered as he pushed me flat on my back and climbed over me. "I have missed you."

I tried to move, to scream. I had to just lie there as he shoved up my top, exposing my breasts.

Fear and nausea churned in my belly as he touched me, kissed me. He didn't let go of one of my breasts as he moved his head down to my scars and he licked each one. A mumble forced its way out of me: "I'm too tired."

He didn't listen or didn't care. He continued to focus on the scars on my stomach with his lips and tongue. Then he ran the tip of his fingers over each one. It was like he was admiring and adoring his work—his marks of possession.

I wanted to scream. I already was in my head, begging myself to move, for someone to help me.

He moved farther down my body and pushed my legs open with his knee. I knew what he was about to do and all I could do was mentally prepare for it.

Tears were finally able to pool in my eyes when he buried his face between my legs. Those tears escaped me, along with a whimper, as he ran his nose over me through my pajama shorts. As he pressed his face against me and inhaled deeply, my chest was heaving up and down rapidly. It was then that I felt that I could scream, and it tore through me. The force behind it was so strong, my throat burned so bad I was sure it was tearing apart.

The feel of someone shaking me and the pain in my throat was what pulled me from my nightmare. I opened my eyes mid-scream, finding Keelan above me. His eyes were wide and his hands were gripping my shoulders. My scream died off at the same time a crash sounded in the room. Keelan let go of me to look behind him, toward the door. Knox had stormed in with Creed and Colt right behind him.

"She was having a nightmare," Keelan said quickly, trying to calm the panic that was all over their faces. They had to have known that I'd been having a nightmare, but given what had happened, I could see why they might have thought my screaming could have been for another reason.

Had it been a nightmare, though? Or my subconscious revealing the truth?

After finding Jacob's body in my house and my gut had been screaming that Mr. X had found me, for a small moment I'd had a sickening thought that my dream of Knox coming to me in the middle of the night not only hadn't been a dream, but it also hadn't been Knox who had climbed into bed with me. I had almost voiced that worry to my guys as well, but things had kept happening and I'd let it go. I'd convinced myself that it had been, in fact, just a dream. It was easier that way because the alternative was too terrible to bear.

I should have known that I wouldn't be so lucky. Maybe seeing Mr. X in the flesh at Desert Stone was what was jogging my memory and making me face the truth.

I felt dirty, as if every inch of my skin had become tainted. What made it worse was that I could still feel the way he'd touched me.

I sobbed in a way that rocked my whole body. I felt so heavy all I could do was roll away from Keelan and slide off the side of the bed to the floor. I wanted to run, to escape my skin, and knowing that was impossible made me feel trapped.

"Baby?" Keelan said and I felt the bed move.

I crawled away, not wanting to be touched. Tears leaked from my eyes as I turned onto my butt and scooted backward until my back ran into the wall. With blurry eyes, I looked from one of my boyfriends to the others.

"Shi?" Creed said as he moved toward me.

"No!" I put my hand out as if to stop him and he froze. My lungs tightened up, making it harder to breathe.

Mr. X must have drugged me. It was why I hadn't been able to wake up the next morning. The more things began to really sink in, a terrifying thought popped into my head. Had Mr. X really stopped when I'd pleaded with him?

"Please... Let's do this tomorrow." Had the promise of sex at a later time convinced him to stop or had he waited until I'd fallen back to sleep to continue?

Had he done more to me?

Did he rape me?

My chest hurt as it heaved. This high-pitched, raspy *hee*

sound came out of me each time I tried to inhale. Not enough air was getting in.

"Shiloh?" Knox said as he took a step forward.

I got on my hands and knees, unable to just sit there. Drops of tears dotted the floor by my hands. "I can't breathe," I quickly forced out with a strangled voice.

Strong arms lifted me off the floor and carried me hurriedly across the room. We were in the bathroom within a blink and by the next I was set on my feet in the shower. Knox turned me to face him, wrapped an arm around me to hold me up as he turned on the shower. Ice-cold water rained down on us, shocking me enough to make me gasp and my lungs expand.

"Breathe," Knox said as he pushed wet hair away from my face.

I took in a deep breath and exhaled it slowly.

"That's it," he praised. "Do it again."

I did it again and again until the water warmed. The more the panic attack receded, the more my body became weak, and I began to tremble. "It wasn't you," I said with a raspy, sore voice. I tilted my head back to stare up at Knox. "It wasn't a dream."

Knox frowned down at me.

More tears leaked from my eyes. "I thought it was you."

Knox brushed water and tears from my cheek. "You thought what was me?"

All I could do was sob.

7

THE SMELL OF COFFEE HAD FILLED THE ROOM. KNOX HAD brewed some and just finished serving everyone each a mugful. Currently, I was sitting at the kitchen island with Colt and Creed sitting on either side of me. Knox and Keelan were both standing in the kitchen, directly across from us. The mood was somber and all four of them wore different faces of upset. That was because I had just gotten done telling them what had happened to me—what Mr. X had done to me.

"Were her clothes..." Keelan started to say as he stared down at his coffee mug in his hand. "When you two went over that morning, did her clothes..." He couldn't bring himself to say it.

"She was dressed," Colt snapped. "The only thing that stood out was that we could barely wake her, and when we did, she was completely out of it."

"The blankets that were hanging off the end of the bed," Creed said as he ran his hand down the side of his face. "The way they were folded over was too precise for them to have been kicked off in her sleep. I remember thinking that it was strange at the time."

"One of us should have stayed with you," Colt said angrily.

"Don't think like that," I grumbled. "If any of you had been there, he might have killed you sooner than he planned."

"Sooner than he planned?" Keelan repeated.

"I was wondering why he hasn't tried to kill us yet," Creed said. "Why go after Isabelle instead of us? We're the bigger threat."

"You're the bigger threat to him because you mean the most to me," I said as I stared down at my barely drunk coffee. "Which is why he was saving you four for last."

"Last?" Colt and Creed said at the same time.

"Mr. X is patient. He stalked me for years. Is it so hard to believe that when he found me again, he would want our reunion to be perfect, or what he feels is perfect? Or did you think that he'd slaughter you and try to take me the moment he found me?" I asked them and their silence was my answer. I let out a humorless laugh. "I knew in my gut something wasn't right. I knew what I was seeing." I shook my head in disdain.

"You're not being fair to yourself," Keelan said.

I scooped up my coffee mug and stood from my seat at the island. "You need to stop letting me off the hook."

As I started to walk away, Colt snapped, "Because you'd rather us tell you it's your fault."

I kept walking, refusing to take the bait.

I heard the sound of a chair scraping along the wood floor before Colt said, "It's tomorrow, Shiloh."

I froze as the meaning of his words hit me. "I've already

had a meltdown once today. Isn't that enough?" I asked over my shoulder.

"You can scream, cry, and break down as much as you need to as long as you're dealing," Colt said.

I didn't have any more tears left to cry today. All I felt inside me right now was anger and none of them deserved that. I took another step forward, intending to retreat to my room.

"You blame yourself for Isabelle." Colt's voice may have been soft when he delivered that blow, but his words packed a powerful punch. It was strong enough to destroy the last bit of control I had.

I whirled around, snarling, "God damn it, Colt!"

Unflinchingly, Colt stood his ground, while the others quietly watched us. I'd expect this kind of pushing from Knox, but ever since I'd explained what Mr. X had done to me while I'd thought it was him, he had been abnormally quiet.

"What happened to Isabelle wasn't your fault," Colt said calmly, yet the firmness in his voice told me his Hulk side was just below the surface.

I shook my head, refusing to listen.

"X is the one—"

I exploded before he could finish. "I know he is! I know it's not my fault he is obsessed with me! I know I did nothing to entice him or make him kill those around me! But I have to take some of the fucking responsibility!" I roared. "As long as he is out there, he is a threat not only to me, but to those around me. I know this and I still fell in love with you! I still let her become my friend!"

"Love is a two-way street, baby girl," Keelan said. "We knew what we were signing up for."

"But Isabelle didn't," I argued.

"You weren't allowed to tell her the truth," Creed said. "And she wanted to be your friend. What were you going to do? Be a bitch to her to keep her away?"

"You're not being fair to yourself," Colt repeated Keelan's words.

"Nothing has been fair for four fucking years!" I yelled as I threw my coffee mug at the front door. It shattered on impact. Ceramic pieces tumbled and slid across the floor and the coffee spilled down the door.

Fisting my hands at my sides, I glared at the floor as I tried to will myself to calm down.

Colt approached me slowly. "I'm sorry about Isabelle." His gentle tone only undid the little amount I was able to calm myself. "But punishing yourself will not undo what happened to her, nor atone for it. And I don't think Isabelle would want you taking on the guilt of it, either," he said.

I shifted my glare from the floor to him.

He stared right back at me with a hard expression. "If that isn't enough to convince you," he added, "then remember that what you do to yourself affects not only you, but us as well."

You suffer, we suffer.

I continued to glare at him as I mulled over his words. With a heavy sigh, I dropped my glare and looked away. "I'm sorry."

Colt closed the distance between us and wrapped his arms around me. One of his hands went to the back of my head before he kissed my temple. "I can't fight your guilt for you, babe, but I can fight it with you," he whispered.

I slid my arms up his back and fisted his shirt. The tears I thought I had run out of began rolling out of my eyes. Not caring that they were soaking his shirt, Colt held me until I found the strength to let go of him.

For a good chunk of the morning, I struggled to deal with what Mr. X had done to me without remembering the way he'd touched me. The sickening part was that I had enjoyed it at the time because I had thought it had been Knox. We had been having issues and he had turned me away when I'd attempted to seduce him in red lingerie. Even though I had been so mad at him for not being honest with me, I had still wanted him—still loved him. So when I had thought he had come to me in the night, touching me like he desired me as much as I desired him, I had been happy and disappointed I'd been too tired to do more with him. Now, I felt like a fool. I felt disgusted, violated. And I couldn't stop feeling Mr. X's hands and mouth on me.

I tried to stay busy, hoping that would help. I went into the room Logan had claimed the last time we'd been here. There was a large safe in his closet. Inside were keys, a rifle, a pistol, stacks of boxes full of bullets, a laptop with an external hard drive sitting on top of it, and my go bag, which I had put in there before leaving for town yesterday.

First, I opened up my go bag and grabbed the burner phone that had Ian's number and Logan's ex-Navy SEAL buddy's number and its charging cord. Next, I grabbed the keys, hard drive, laptop, and its power cord. Out in the living room, Colt, Creed, and Keelan were sitting around looking bored.

I handed the laptop, power cord, and hard drive to Creed. "There isn't any internet, but there's a bunch of movies on this hard drive." I handed the keys to Keelan. "These are to the basement and the shed. You'll find the entrance to the basement outside on the side of the cabin near the log pile. Down there is a small gym and a bunch of board games. The shed has outdoor stuff like fishing gear." All of the things I mentioned had been left behind by the previous owner, who according to the realtor was an elderly lady who'd used to vacation up here with her husband and their family multiple times a year before her husband had passed away. Now that her husband was gone, she hadn't wanted the property anymore and had sold the place with pretty much everything inside. The realtor had told Logan that it was because she hadn't wanted to deal with the hassle of moving, which worked out for us perfectly.

"Where's Knox?" I asked them.

"He went for a walk," Creed answered as he got up to plug in the laptop.

I looked toward the front door, wondering if he was all right. He had been too quiet this morning, even when we'd all eaten breakfast together. I had been so busy dealing with my own demons all morning, I hadn't taken the time to ask what was wrong.

Deciding to check on him when he got back, I went into my room and plugged in the burner phone to charge it. Wanting to stay busy, I collected all the stuff I would need to change my hair from where I'd put it on my dresser yesterday and headed to the bathroom.

About an hour and a crap-ton of foil later, I stood in front of the mirror waiting. My sections and foil technique would never get me hired at a salon, but for a home job it didn't look too bad. According to the instructions, I couldn't leave the bleach in my hair for more than thirty minutes. I really,

really hoped I didn't fry my hair. I could live with traffic-cone-colored hair so long as I didn't have to chop it all off. I turned my head side to side, trying to envision it. "Orange might actually look good on me."

I huffed a laugh and folded my arms across my chest. Hair was such a trivial thing to worry over given everything else that was going on. Maybe I should take this type of worry as a reprieve.

I glanced at the time on the burner phone I'd been able to charge for a short time. Seeing that it had been thirty minutes, I took a deep breath and began unfolding a foil piece from my hair. The moment my small chunk of hair was revealed, I stopped breathing.

My hair was not fried.

My hair was not orange.

"No," I gasped and began ripping foils out. Each chunk of hair that was unveiled was the same. I didn't know how long I stood there, shocked. I gripped the edge of the sink, debating what I should do. I needed to rinse the product out, but I was considering keeping it in, hoping it would make what I was seeing go away.

I wished I had my phone so I could look up what to do.

I let out a frustrated noise and went to turn on the shower. As I washed my hair, I tried to convince myself that I was seeing things. I refused to look in the mirror when I got out. Instead, I wrapped my hair up in a towel and went to go get dressed first.

I returned to the bathroom, praying to any deity who would listen that my hair would be orange. Steeling myself for what I knew was to come, I pulled the towel from my hair.

Wet, pink strands fell to my shoulders.

I will not cry over hair. I will not cry over hair.

With a clenched jaw, I plugged in the hairdryer I had just bought during our trip to town and began drying my hair. By the time I was done, I felt…I felt a lot. Sadness was the stronger emotion weighing on me, because I didn't see myself in the mirror. I saw Shayla.

Her hair had been a light cotton-candy pink, but mine was a little bit darker. It was more of a pink rose color, but it was close enough to play tricks on my eyes. When said eyes began to burn, I forced myself to look away. To avoid the temptation, I left the bathroom and went to sit on the edge of my bed.

What a terrible day, I thought as I lay back. *What a handful of terrible days.*

Terrible was an understatement.

I wanted to go for a run. The type of run that would make me feel sore for days. I wanted to feel that hurt. I almost craved it. Because it was a bearable, controlled type of pain, unlike everything I was feeling right now. Disappointment was the only thing holding me back. My guys' disappointment. Dr. Bolton's disappointment. My disappointment.

I just needed a break from the overwhelming weight I was carrying. Just one tiny break.

8

I ENDURED LYING THERE FOR A WHOLE FIVE MINUTES BEFORE I had to get up and get busy. Why? Because my mind drifted to Mr. X again and the urge to rip off my skin just to remove the feel of him nearly sent me over the edge of insanity. And if I let myself reach that point, I really would backslide.

It was dinnertime. I honestly was not in the mood to cook, which just showed how messed-up I was feeling.

For my sanity, I pushed myself toward the door. As I reached to open it, I froze when my eyes caught on the ends of my hair.

I had never not wanted to be in my body more than I did right then. Gritting my teeth, I grabbed the brown knitted beanie I'd worn to town yesterday and put it on. After stuffing all of my hair into it, I left my room.

All four of my guys were hanging out in the living room. They went quiet as I entered, and I could feel them watching me as I headed to the kitchen.

"I'm guessing your hair didn't turn out the way you wanted," Colt said as I opened the fridge.

"No." The curt word fell from my lips before I could even remind myself not to take out my frustration on them. I looked around in the fridge as I went over in my head what to make. I pulled out everything I'd need to make a simple baked chicken meal. As I set everything on the counter, I felt one of them come over.

"Shi," Creed said from right behind me. "Is this another sweatshirt situation?"

I stiffened for a breath before turning to face him. "No." This time, I was able to soften my voice before speaking.

Frowning, he reached toward my head.

I moved without thought. My hand shot out to block him from touching my beanie and I stepped out of his reach. "I love you, but I will ground you," I warned angrily.

Keelan chuckled in the living room as he watched us.

Creed's frown shifted into a smirk. "It can't be that bad."

I didn't respond. The last thing I wanted to do was pique his curiosity more. Unfortunately, the determined glint in his eye told me it was too late. He wouldn't back off.

"You can't wear a hat forever, Shi. You might as well rip off the Band-Aid now and get it over with," he said.

Unless I really wanted to put my boyfriend on his butt and risk hurting him, I really only had one option. "Would you still find me attractive if I was bald?" Only reason I asked was because I was seriously feeling the impulse to take scissors to my hair. I wouldn't, though. What I was feeling would pass. I just had to keep reminding myself of that.

"Yes," they all said without hesitation.

I sighed. "You all said that a little too quickly," I grumbled as I moved over to the cabinet that held the pots and pans. I grabbed a skillet and as I set it on the stove, I felt

Creed come up behind me. He grabbed my beanie. I closed my eyes as it was removed, and my hair fell to my shoulders.

The reaction I got was silence. They knew I didn't like pink, and they knew why.

"For what it's worth, you look beautiful," Creed said sullenly.

I couldn't bring myself to say thank you. I couldn't even move my hands to cook. I was so uncomfortable in my body that I wanted to tap out so badly. I wanted to run so badly. If there had been any alcohol here, I was pretty sure I'd be already chugging it. All I could do in that moment was stand there, staring down at the stove, battling with myself.

Move, Shiloh.

Just keep moving.

It's terrible right now.

It'll pass.

It'll pass.

"Babe?" Colt said at the same time Knox said, "Shiloh?"

Creed grabbed me by my shoulders and spun me around to face him. His eyes bounced all over my face. He must have seen something that unsettled him, because he pulled me to his chest and wrapped his arms around me.

I tried to lift my hands from my sides to hug him back. They felt so heavy that I only got as far as his waist. "Can someone help me cook?" I asked as I pushed on his hips a little.

"I'll help," Knox said as he came into the kitchen.

I can do this.

I can keep moving.

Creed unwrapped his arms from around me, but didn't move or look away from me.

Knox came up next to us. "I got this, Creed," he assured his little brother and a look passed between them.

Creed reluctantly backed away, letting go of me completely.

Knox took his place in front of me. The intensity of his stare and the way he towered over me made me feel like he was blocking out the rest of the world. Knox was the strongest out of the five of us. I found myself leaning toward him and resting my forehead against his chest, hoping to absorb a little bit of his strength.

He ran his hand down the back of my head to cup the back of my neck. "Are you even hungry?"

I shook my head against him.

"Okay." He kissed the top of my head before moving away.

I watched him grab the food I'd taken out and put it all back in the fridge. Then he took my hand. I let him pull me and lead me back to my room.

As soon as we got inside, I asked, "What about dinner?"

He let go of my hand. "They're big boys. They can feed themselves," he said as he shut the door and leaned against it with his arms folded over his chest.

I moved farther into the room. "If you brought me in here to ask me what's wrong or to talk—"

"I don't need to ask," he cut me off.

I went to go sit on the edge of the bed. "Then why did you bring me in here?"

"You're struggling."

I scoffed as I shook my head. "I'm doing everything I can not to make past mistakes. I know I slipped and buried things, but that was so I could get us all here—somewhere safe."

"I didn't bring you in here to lecture you," he said. "You haven't done anything wrong. I can see you're itching to go running. I can also see that you're fighting it."

"Is that why you brought me in here? To help talk me off the ledge?"

"I brought you in here to ask what you need to help you," he grumbled. "It's been one nightmare after another for days and you've had to deal with the brunt of it."

"I would shoulder all the nightmares if I could." Even if it destroyed me, if I could shield them from it all, I would.

By the angry frown that adorned his face, I was almost convinced he was a mind reader for a second. "That's not how this works."

"And how does this work?" I asked him.

"We shoulder it together," he said. "So what do you need?"

"I don't know." If I knew how to make myself feel better, I would have done it by now.

"Would it help to talk about things, then?"

I didn't really see the point. He knew why my hair bothered me and he'd gotten all the details this morning about Mr. X. Speaking of this morning... "Why were you so quiet this morning?"

"You're deflecting."

"Maybe I'd be more forthcoming if you were, too," I shot back.

He was quiet for a moment as he clearly debated. "I was angry."

"Because I thought it was you?"

The way he clenched his jaw gave me my answer.

I looked away and steeled myself for what I had to ask

next. "You're angry with me because I couldn't tell the difference?"

"No." He practically growled.

I winced a little and made myself stare back at him.

He was watching me with a hard frown. "I'm angry that he assaulted you period. Yes, it upset me that you thought it was me. Not because I'm offended you would ever think I would sneak over and be with you like that. After you had come over earlier that day and unwrapped yourself like a fucking present, I wanted to say fuck it and go to you that night. I wish I had instead of denying myself, because meanwhile that fucker…"

Knox trailed off, his face downcast. His expression was downright murderous and the muscles in his jaw ticked. I stayed quiet as he calmed himself.

"I absolutely do not fault you for thinking that it was me. It could have been. I'm upset at how much he got away with because you didn't know."

It took a minute to process what he'd said. "If I hadn't thought it was you, he would have raped me right then and there. If I hadn't thought it was you and I'd realized it was him, I would have freaked out and tried to fight. Because I thought it was you, I reacted as he's always wanted me to react to him. Like a girlfriend who didn't want to turn him away, but was too tired for what he wanted, and asked if we could do it the next day. Because I thought it was you, I fed into his fantasy and prevented something that would be a lot harder to come back from."

This time he was quiet as he processed. He didn't look happy, but he was less upset.

"I hate my hair," I said because it was my turn to be forthcoming. "I don't see myself when I look in the mirror. I see Shayla. You would think I would be happy to see her. It's why I started dyeing my hair to begin with. To hold onto her. To see glimpses of her. But those small glimpses I used to get were memories. Good ones. Looking into the mirror now, all I can see are her last moments. I see her dead." I clasped my hands together tightly in my lap. "And since I woke up this morning, I can't stop feeling the way *he* touched me. I've been trying to keep busy. To move around. If I'm moving, I can try to process things without feeling him. But the moment I slow down, he takes over and I want to rip off my skin. I quite literally hate my body from head to toe and I feel trapped because of that."

"We can change your hair. I'll go to town tomorrow—"

"We should avoid going to town unless we absolutely need to," I said.

The corner of his mouth lifted slightly. "We'll cover up all the mirrors until then."

"I guess that solves that," I said dryly and that made him smile a little bit more. Unfortunately, I made that smile disappear when I added, "I don't think you'll be able to help me with the rest. Unless you're able to erase my memories, I don't think I'll be able to stop feeling him."

He contemplated for a bit. "I can only give you new memories."

"Only good ones, please," I said as I lay back on the bed.

"How good do you want them?"

It took me a few seconds to realize what he was asking. Gaping, I turned my head to the side so I could look at him.

"I can't erase what he did, but if you're comfortable with it, I can help you forget him for a little while," he said.

"I thought using sex as a distraction was bad."

"It is bad if you're using it to completely avoid dealing.

You're overwhelmed to the point of breaking because all you've been doing is facing shit that has been thrown at you today. You're allowed a break."

For a split second, I felt dirty, like I was damaged somehow and he was only wanting to have sex with me to fix me. Then I quickly imagined lighting that toxic thought on fire. Knox loved me and he would never sleep with me for just the sake of helping me. "Is this really how you want our first time to be?"

"I would offer to go get one of my brothers, but I don't think I can leave you right now."

I pushed up on my elbows. "Why?"

His eyes locked with mine and I could see that he was struggling to contain his anger. "I don't like that he touched you," he said as if that explained why.

It didn't. At least, not at first, but then I remembered his reasons why he hadn't come to me the night Mr. X had. The hang-up in our relationship had been his worry of jealousy. He had been unsure if he could share me with his brothers. Since then, we had learned he could. However, someone other than his brothers had touched me.

"You're feeling possessive."

He sighed through his nose. "Yes and no. I know that makes me a fucking bastard, but you're mine. Someone hurt you when you should've been with me, and I can't fucking stand it."

I opened my mouth to argue that it hadn't been his fault when he said, "I know, Shiloh."

If he knew, then why did he sound so angry with himself? Then I realized what I was seeing. I wondered how we'd swapped places. Normally, I was the one who was too riddled with guilt to see reason.

I didn't know why, but I was fighting not to smile. Since it had been days since the last time I'd smiled, there was a possibility I'd gone mad. Or maybe it was because it was stupidly wonderful to be on this side of things. To see, feel, and understand my guys' perspectives instead of imagining them.

I got to my feet, determined to battle his guilt with him and to help satiate his possessive side. Not just for him, but for myself, too. I wanted that break he offered, badly. To be honest, he had already granted me it and I wasn't ready for it to end.

"We don't have to do anything. I can just hold you..."

He trailed off when I reached for the bottom of my sweater and took it off. I wasn't wearing anything underneath. Not even a bra. I walked toward him as I unbuttoned my pants. I stopped to shove them down. He pushed away from the door and knelt before me to help remove my jeans from my knees down. I put my hands on his shoulders so I wouldn't fall as I stepped out of each pant leg and then my socks.

Standing in front of him in nothing but pale blue underwear, my heart started to race. A small part of me wished I had chosen to wear something a little bit sexier. Unfortunately, all I had here was plain bras and panties, apart from the superhero lingerie I'd traveled here in.

Knox tossed my jeans and socks to the side and his intense, gorgeous, golden-brown eyes moved up my body, starting at my feet. His hands cupped the backs of my calves and traveled up with his gaze. As his warm palms smoothed up the backs of my thighs, he leaned forward, pressing his lips to my lower stomach just above the top of my panties.

He let go of my thighs to hook his fingers into the sides of my underwear and slid it off.

His mouth never left my lower stomach as he helped me remove the last scrap of clothing I wore. He kissed me from hip to hip and as soon as I was totally naked, that mouth drifted south. He took his time as he made his journey down and I found myself pushing up to my tiptoes wanting to speed things along.

He huffed a laugh over my sex when he realized what I was doing. Grasping the backs of my thighs just below my butt cheeks, he smirked up at me. "You're impatient."

I squeezed his shoulders. "How patient would you be if I was kneeling—"

My words were cut off when his hands slid up to my butt cheeks as his mouth came down on top of my clit. His fingers gripped me firmly as he brought his tongue into play by stroking it through the folds of my pussy.

Gasping, my hands went to the back of his head. I tried not to hold him too tightly, but my legs were beginning to shake. They nearly gave out when he started flicking that tongue on my clit. "Knox," I whimpered.

He pulled away and stood, forcing my hands to drop from behind his head. His mouth found mine and I could taste myself on his tongue as he stroked it along mine.

Without breaking our kiss, he lifted me into his arms bridal-style and carried me across the room. He put a knee on the bed so that he could lay me down with a gentleness that I wasn't expecting. I pulled away to meet his eyes to see what he was thinking. To my surprise, the intensity I normally felt when he stared at me seemed different. It wasn't any less intense. It just wasn't sharp. It had softened. Was this what he looked like behind his many, many shields?

I'd known after the first few times interacting with him that I would never be worthy in his eyes just based on my character alone. To see this side of him, I had to withstand the way he challenged and pushed. I saw it for what it was, and I hadn't backed down. I never would.

Holding himself up with one arm on the mattress by my head, his eyes narrowed a little. "What is it?"

I cupped his face and leaned up to give him a quick kiss. "I love you."

His brows rose a little. "I know."

Way to pop my lovey-dovey bubble. "You know?"

An annoying smirk graced his gorgeous face as he moved his head down and kissed me over my heart. "I do."

"I take it back," I grumbled.

I felt him smile against my chest before he moved down a little more and took my nipple into his mouth.

A little moan slipped out of me as he sucked, but it was quickly cut off with a hiss when he tugged on my sensitive peak with his teeth. I felt his fingers trail up my thigh just before they dove between my legs.

"You can't take it back," he said as his fingers slid through the wetness that had pooled at my core.

"Yes, I can," I breathed.

Knox pushed two fingers inside me, and I grabbed ahold of his shoulder as I savored the feeling of being stretched.

"Are you saying you don't love me?" he asked as he withdrew those fingers and pushed them back in.

I didn't respond. Instead, I just focused on the way he was moving his fingers in and out of me. Wanting to come, my hips moved to meet the thrust of his fingers.

Knox lifted away from my breast so he could stare down

between my legs. "Still so impatient." He began rubbing his thumb over my clit, making me groan.

"We'll see how patient you are the next time I have my hand wrapped—ah!"

Knox's fingers inside me curled upward as he moved them inside me, hitting that perfect spot. Feeling that addictive pressure begin to build from what he was doing, my hips jutted up as if to beg him not to stop. He didn't.

"Still a brat, even with my fingers buried deep in your pussy." Having a filthy mouth was undoubtedly a Stone trait.

"You love it," I whined.

"That my fingers are buried in this tight, pink pussy?" he said with a smirk. "I suppose I do."

"Knox!" I growled-slash-groaned with my eyes squeezed shut. I was so close to the precipice of coming.

He chuckled as he trailed kisses down my sternum to my belly button. "You're close, Shiloh."

"Yes," I whimpered. My orgasm was right there, about to take over my body just as his mouth moved over to my scars next to my belly button. Within an instant, all the buildup to my climax disappeared and every inch of me went still. Mr. X flashed in my mind, and I wasn't feeling Knox touching me anymore.

"Look at me." Knox's firm voice pulled me from my thoughts and made me open my eyes. I stared down my body to see him kneeling between my legs, fingers inside me, and his mouth hovering inches above my scars. His eyes locked with mine. "I'm the one with you right now. Not him. He will never touch you like this again."

I released a shaky breath to calm myself.

"Keep your eyes on me and you'll only see me," he said,

and he reached for my hand. He brought it to the side of his face. "Feel me."

His hand dropped from mine, and I kept my hand against his cheek as he leaned down toward my scars. I held my breath, watching him as he laid a kiss on one scar, then the other. When he didn't disappear, I exhaled.

"Still with me?" he asked.

I ran the tips of my fingers over the scruff along his jaw before moving them up and through his hair. "Yes."

Knox's mouth moved down and before I knew it, his tongue replaced where his thumb had been circling my clit.

Moaning, my head fell back against the mattress.

"If you want to come, you need to keep watching me, Shiloh," he said and began flicking his tongue in a way that made me lift my hips and push down on his head.

I shook my head against the mattress. "Please."

He pulled away from my clit.

I let out a frustrated growl and lifted my head to look down at him.

"Don't take your eyes off me."

I did as he asked because I knew what he was doing—what he was hoping to achieve. He not only was making sure I knew that he was the one touching me, but he was also trying to give me something better to remember. Good memories to fight the bad.

Knox stared right back at me as his tongue flicked out. It was probably the hottest thing I'd ever seen. With his fingers pumping in and out of me and his tongue attacking my clit, I felt release hurtling toward me.

"Do you love me?" he asked me just before I was about to come.

"Yes!" I cried out, deliriously mad he'd stopped.

The instant he returned his tongue to my clit, I shattered. Spots dotted my vision and I dropped my head back to the mattress.

Knox pulled his fingers from me and climbed off the bed. Trying to catch my breath, I watched him with hooded eyes as he removed his clothes. When he was standing in front of me in all his naked glory, I couldn't take my eyes off him.

He wrapped his hand around the base of his cock. "Open your legs for me."

My knees were currently bent and together. Suddenly feeling a little nervous, I bit my lip and slowly opened them, revealing myself to him.

His eyes danced all over my body, greedily taking in every inch of me as he stroked his cock. "So beautiful."

I snapped my legs closed. "Stop staring."

He chuckled as he reached for the nightstand drawer and pulled out a condom. "I just had my tongue in the place you're trying to hide. How could you possibly feel shy?"

I watched as he ripped open the condom packet and rolled it on. "Because you're just standing there staring at me," I said.

"I've been waiting a long time for this moment." He climbed back up on the bed and grasped my knees. "I plan on doing more than just staring at you."

He pushed my legs apart and climbed up the rest of my body until his hips were cradled between my thighs. Leaning down from where he was holding himself above me, he pressed his lips to mine. I ran my hands up his large chest and over the muscles of his shoulders.

"Are you ready?" he asked me as he reached a hand between us.

That question made my heart pound with anticipation. "Yes."

He aligned with my entrance and pushed into me slowly. My breath hitched and I squeezed his shoulders as I stretched around him.

When he was fully inside me, he let out a curse. "I want to be gentle with you, but fuck."

I smiled. "I know you're a big strong man and all, but I've told you before, you can't break my vagina."

He just blinked at me.

"I mean, you're welcome to try and—"

Knox cut me off by pulling out of me and slamming back in. I let out a whimper.

He seemed to enjoy the sound and continued to thrust into me. "Is this the trick to get you to behave?" he asked as he placed kisses down my neck. "I have to fuck the brat out of you?"

I wanted to rebel and say something smart back at him, but only moans left my lips.

He let out a deep chuckle and sat up. His big hands went to my hips and he lifted up my pelvis off the bed. Holding my waist up, he continued to thrust into me. The new angle allowed him to enter me deeper and to rub me in places that lit the fuse that would lead to my release. I arched and writhed my upper body against the mattress and blankets beneath me.

He pulled on my hips to meet his every thrust, making me cry out every time. The grunt-like growl that came out of him as he watched where our bodies joined made my toes curl. "Fuck. You take me so well." His deep, rumbling words sounded pleased.

"I'm going to come," I whined.

"Who's going to make you come?" he demanded.

I fisted the blankets on the bed and forced out the word, "You."

"Who's inside your pussy right now?"

I moaned as I arched my back even higher as I felt myself reaching the peak. "You!"

"That's right, Shiloh," he said. "Me. Not him. Me. He will never have you. You will never be his. You belong to us."

It was a promise—a vow that was underlined with a threat. Mr. X wasn't just a serial killer in his eyes, but a man who touched what didn't belong to him.

Knox's claim detonated me and I came screaming.

As I contracted around him, he slammed us together hard, burying himself deep inside me. He groaned as his cock swelled and his release spilled out of him. His hands slid up my back and he lifted me up to straddle him. The moment we were chest to chest, I wrapped my arms around his neck and held onto him as my soul returned to my body.

9

THE SOUND OF THE BEDROOM DOOR OPENING WAS WHAT WOKE me. I thought it was Knox leaving or one of his brothers coming into the room. When I heard the sound of boots walking on the wood floor next, getting closer and closer to the side of the bed where I was lying, I knew I'd assumed wrong.

I opened my eyes and just barely could see a shadow standing over me. I knew who it was and fear made my body too heavy to move.

In the darkness, I faintly saw him reach for me before his hand wrapped around my throat. As soon as he began choking me, I was able to move my arms and I grabbed ahold of his arm to try to stop him. It was no use, though. I fought to suck in air, but none reached my lungs. I smacked, punched, and pushed at him to no avail.

Knox! *I internally screamed for him. He was sound asleep next to me, completely unaware of what was happening. Tears leaked from the corners of my eyes, knowing that if Mr. X rendered me unconscious, he'd kill Knox next.*

"You...are..." Mr. X leaned down, bringing us face to face. *"Mine!" he roared over my mouth.*

I'm not yours! *I wanted to scream, but I could feel myself slipping away into nothingness.*

I woke gasping for air. The room was full of light; it was morning.

An arm tightened around my middle, pulling me closer to a chest. Knox's voice filled my ear. "I have you. You're safe."

I rolled over and buried my face in his bare chest.

His hand went to the back of my neck and began kneading it. "Do you want to talk about it?"

"I don't dream about the night my family was killed anymore," I said. "All I dream about is him finding us. In Arizona. Here. I fear losing the four of you more than anything and my nightmares have realized that."

Knox was quiet for a while and if he hadn't been massaging the back of my neck, I would have thought he'd fallen asleep. "I could make promises that I would do everything in my power to make sure he doesn't hurt you again, but I think that would just stress you out."

"You're right. I'd rather protect you."

He sighed. "My little control-freak-slash-hero."

I leaned back to look up at him and he stared down at me with a tired smirk. "You're my family, Knox," I said. "You, Keelan, Colt, and Creed. The four of you are my family. I love you so much that I'd endure a lifetime of nightmares so long as the four of you were safe."

His eyes became more awake the more I spoke. "Do you

think that we don't feel the same? That I don't want to kill him for what he's done to you?" His hand stopped massaging the back of my neck and instead just gripped me, holding me in place. "I've never felt this type of rage before you. The mere thought of anyone hurting you..." He trailed off with a clenched jaw. It clearly angered him just talking about it. "My need to protect you is just as great as yours. Never doubt that."

I pushed on his shoulder until he rolled onto his back and I climbed on top of him. "I don't doubt it." Straddling his hips, I was reminded that we had fallen asleep naked last night, and I was currently sitting on what felt like a hard rod.

Knox gave me a little bit of déjà vu when he put an arm behind his head. Instead of just staring up at me, he reached up and tucked my hair behind my ear. "I love you."

Every thought, everything I'd planned on saying when I'd climbed on top of him, left my head. He hadn't said that when he thought I'd been sleeping. He'd just told me that he loved me without fear, without shields, without pressure. He'd said it purely because that was what he felt and because he wanted to, and it was profound.

I leaned down and just before I kissed him, I said, "I know."

The smile that stretched his mouth was almost too beautiful to ruin with a kiss. Almost. As I pressed my lips to his, I promised to myself that I'd find another reason to make him smile like that again.

When I left my room that morning, I felt lighter. I still hated my hair, and it was going to stay in a messy bun until I was able to change it, but it no longer gutted me to see it. As for everything else, I wasn't as overwhelmed by it, or rather, the break Knox had given me had allowed me to recoup my mental and emotional strength to withstand my demons.

The thought of cooking breakfast didn't seem like such a battle as I pulled things out of the fridge. Knox and I had skipped dinner last night. I was starving and I was sure he was as well.

The cabin was quiet, but it was fairly early in the morning. Keelan and the twins were probably still sleeping.

Knox and I worked quietly together in the kitchen. The delicious smells of coffee and food quickly filled the room, drawing Keelan out of bed first. I was currently mixing pancake batter at the island as he came out of the closest bedroom.

Yawning, he came to me and kissed the top of my head. "How are you feeling?"

"Better." Just as I said that, I got a really sharp cramp that made me grab the edge of the island and hunch over a little. I had started my period this morning at the most inconvenient and embarrassing time.

After Knox had said he loved me, we'd started kissing. That kissing had turned into sex. He'd had my legs on his shoulders and pounded into me until release hit us both. It had been quick, hard, and satisfying. Every part of that moment had been wonderful. That was, until Knox had pulled out of me and seen my monthly visitor had finally showed up.

I had felt Knox still as he'd stared down between us. "Did I hurt you?"

"No. Why?" I had responded, propping myself up on my elbows to see what he had been looking at. Within a second

I'd switched from hugely relieved to mortified. I'd quickly covered his eyes with my hands. "Oh my God! Don't look!"

Knox had been calm. "I already saw. It's nothing to be embarrassed about." He'd pulled my hands from his eyes. A small frown had taken over his face when he'd seen my face. I hadn't been able to hide that I'd not only been embarrassed, but about to freak out. As if completely unbothered, he had scooped me up, carried me to the bathroom, and we'd taken a shower together.

Keelan put a hand on my shoulder, pulling me back to the present. "What's wrong?" he asked.

I quickly straightened and went back to whisking the clumps out of the pancake batter. "Nothing."

"She has cramps," Knox said from where he stood at the stove cooking bacon.

Understanding showed on Keelan's face. "Do you need anything?"

"Nope," I said as I went over to the large pantry cabinet next to the fridge. "You don't mind having chocolate-chip pancakes for breakfast, do you?" I grabbed one of the bags of chocolate chips I'd picked up in town and returned to my mixing bowl of batter.

Keelan was pouring himself a cup of coffee when he answered, "I don't think anyone in this family will mind a little bit of chocolate with their breakfast."

I was happy that he was all right with having chocolate-chip pancakes. However, I was irritated by the word *little*. Sure, half a bag would be the normal batter to chip ratio, but today…

I ripped open one end of the bag and the smell of chocolaty goodness filled my nose. It smelled so good my mouth watered. I plucked a chip from the bag and popped it into my mouth. It seemed to melt instantly on my tongue, and I let out a tiny moan-slash-*mmm*. I ate a couple more chips before dumping the whole bag into the batter and I felt zero remorse about doing it.

Feeling like I was being watched, I glanced over my shoulder. Keelan and Knox were staring at me, surprised.

"Oh no. I accidentally dumped the whole bag in." My words came out flat and it was blatantly obvious that I was lying. I gave them a look that dared them to call me out on it.

Knox looked like he was fighting not to smile and turned back to face the stove.

Keelan did nothing to hide his smile. "If I'd known chocolate made you moan like that, I would have insisted a long time ago that we had it with every breakfast."

Heat blooming in my cheeks, I turned back toward the island and started mixing the chips into the batter. "Why just breakfast?" The question slipped out before I could stop myself.

Keelan came up behind me and he pressed his lips where my neck met my shoulder, making me shiver a little. "I have two reasons," he said and kissed me again, this time higher up on my neck. "One: hearing you moan first thing in the morning is the best way to start my day. It would be better if I was the one making you moan, but I'll enjoy the sound any way I can hear it." His lips moved up and he dragged his teeth along the sensitive spot just below my ear, which made my sock-covered toes curl against the floor. "And two: my life would become very unproductive if I heard you moaning all day." His voice deepened as he spoke.

I found myself tilting my head to the side like an offering. "And why is that?"

He grabbed one of my hands and placed it over his cock.

Through his pajama pants, I could feel that he was hard. "Those sexy noises are kryptonite to my self-control." One of his hands grabbed me by the hip while the other found its way up my shirt. His fingers felt warm as they slid across my stomach. "If I'm exposed to too much, you'll find yourself on your back or bent over with my cock buried inside you."

Cheese and rice! I had to grab the edge of the counter for a whole new reason. "It's not nice to tease," I said with an affected voice.

"I'm not teasing." He licked the shell of my ear. "Say the word and I'll bend you over this counter right now. I bet we can wake the twins when I make you come screaming."

"I'm on my period, Keelan."

I felt him shake with silent laughter behind me. "You say that as if that will deter me from fucking you."

"Keelan," I admonished.

He chuckled. "Wasn't it you that said a dirty time sounded like a fun time?"

"I was talking about the mud run."

"The same could be said in this case," he said, and I could hear the smile in his voice.

I moved to the side before completely walking away from him and out of the kitchen. "Knox, the pancake batter is made. I'm going to go wake up Colt and Creed."

"All right," Knox said, his voice light as if he was trying not to laugh.

Keelan didn't even try to stop himself. I could hear him chuckling until I made it to the room Colt and Creed were sleeping in.

I didn't bother knocking before I entered. I went straight in. Colt and Creed were sharing a queen bed. Colt woke as soon as I entered, but Creed didn't even stir.

"Hey," Colt said tiredly as I climbed up onto the foot of the bed and crawled between them.

Creed's eyes opened a little as soon as I lay down and he wrapped his arm across my stomach.

I tensed up slightly.

"What's wrong?" Creed asked.

"I'm not pregnant." It was meant to be a joke, but as soon as I said that, I realized I had just unloaded a worry I'd been holding onto.

"What?" Creed said at the same time Colt said, "Did you think you were pregnant?"

Crap.

"I was a few days late," I admitted as I sat up and scooted back toward the foot of the bed. "I had a feeling stress was the reason I wasn't getting it. I have a history of being late due to stress."

Colt sat up. "You weren't having sex back then, though."

"No wonder you went pale when we went into the tampon aisle the other day," Creed grumbled as he climbed out of bed. "Why didn't you say anything?"

Inwardly, I was chastising myself for bringing it up. "You were upset with me," I said, retreating backward toward the door. "Anyway, it's not an issue anymore. I got my period. Let's go eat breakfast." I spun on my heel, hoping that they would let the topic go.

"Shi," Creed called out to me at the same time Colt said, "Babe."

I made it a few steps into the hall when I felt both of them catch up behind me.

"If you ever think you're pregnant," Creed said, "I don't care how upset I am, tell me. Yell it at me if you feel the need to."

I froze just as I entered the living room. Creed's voice had been loud enough for even Keelan and Knox to hear, because both of their heads whipped in our direction.

"What?" Keelan gaped.

As Creed would say, *Cheese and fucking rice!*

I turned to face Creed and Colt. "The main reason I didn't say anything was because there was so much going on that I couldn't mentally take it on, and to talk about it would not only force me to, but it would have caused you to worry as well. None of us needed that added stress. I figured it'd be best to wait a week or two and if I still didn't start my period, then it would be time to worry."

"That makes sense," Colt said.

Creed sighed. "I don't like that you felt like you couldn't say anything to me."

"She knows to yell at you next time," Colt said. "Let's move on from this."

"Let's hope there isn't a next time," I said and turned around with the intent to head to the kitchen, but Keelan was standing right behind me.

"You thought you were pregnant?" he asked.

I let out a sigh and went on to explain.

Keelan and Knox were quiet as I spoke, and when I finished, Keelan put his hands on my shoulders. "Creed's right. If you ever think you're pregnant, tell us."

"And then what?" Knox asked as he walked over.

"What do you mean *and then what?*" Creed asked.

Knox stared at his younger brothers. "We haven't talked about Shiloh possibly getting pregnant. Condoms and contraceptives aren't one hundred percent. So it could happen."

"If she does, she does," Creed said like it wasn't a big deal.

Knox frowned at Creed. "A baby is a huge responsibility and something not all of us are on board with."

Creed frowned back at his oldest brother. "Why are you saying that when you know that if we got Shi pregnant, we'd be fine with it? Sure, it'd be scary at first, but I don't think even you would be opposed to adding to our family. We would figure it out."

"I'm not talking about the four of us," Knox said, and his gaze shifted to me.

Feeling the weight of all of their eyes, I looked down. "I'm not on board with it."

Keelan's hands moved from my shoulders to cup my face. "That's all right, baby girl." He made me look up at him. "This conversation isn't to make you feel ashamed. It's just to know where we all stand if it ever happens."

Colt put his hand on my lower back. "What about in the future, babe? When the time is right, would you want kids then?"

"I'm too scared to think about the future," I said. Before Mr. X had found me in Arizona, I'd actually thought I could allow myself to envision a future. And now, I looked back at myself from a week ago and thought how stupid I had been. "As long as Mr. X is alive, I can't let myself. It will only lead to disappointment, because his sole purpose is to rip away any future I might want, and he's proven that he can."

"What about before X came into your life?" Creed asked. "You told me once that you wanted to be a chef like your mother. Did you want anything else out of life before he ruined it?"

That question was too painful to answer. I grabbed

Keelan's wrists and pulled them from my face. "It doesn't matter what I wanted back then, Creed."

"Even though you feel like you can't envision a future, you must still want something to keep moving forward," Colt prompted.

For a second, I felt like deflecting, but I knew that wouldn't work on them. I sighed and gave them the soul-baring truth. "After Mr. X killed my family, the only thing I wanted out of this life was to know what it was like to feel happy again. You four came into my life and gave me that."

"Hearing that just made me equally happy and sad, baby girl," Keelan said.

"Some people go their whole lives without knowing happiness. Mine is multiplied by four," I told him and headed toward the kitchen to finish cooking breakfast.

10

THREE DAYS WENT BY. IT SNOWED A LOT, WHICH MY GUYS who were born and raised in the desert weren't used to. The awe on their faces at what looked like a winter wonderland outside and the fun we all had playing in it was uplifting. Snowmen were built. Snowball fights were fought. In the evenings we lit cozy fires. We played board games from the collection in the basement and watched movies on the computer. Those three days were as perfect as could be under the circumstances and I was grateful for it. If I could have encapsulated it, I would have, or at least taken some pictures.

Today was a slightly warmer day. Just after breakfast, I grabbed one of my rifles I'd brought with me from Arizona and a box of bullets from the safe. I was more experienced with pistols; shooting a rifle was something I could use more practice with.

Knox and Keelan were down in the basement using the small gym. As I was going through the trash for cans from last night's dinner, Colt and Creed came into the kitchen to see what I was up to.

"What are you doing, Shi?" Creed asked as he leaned against the kitchen island.

I set the third can I'd found on the counter. "Looking for cans to shoot."

"You're going shooting?" Colt asked with interest underlining his voice.

I glanced at the two of them. They were both eyeing the rifle and box of bullets that I'd laid across the kitchen island.

"Want to learn how to shoot a rifle?" I asked Colt and Creed.

"Sure," they said at the same time.

After getting bundled up in warm coats, gloves, and boots, we left to search the property for a good spot. We found a knocked-over tree in a clearing. After widely lining up the cans across it, I put a good amount of distance between us and the tree. "Here should be good." I placed myself between them so they could see me and my rifle.

"I have a bolt-action rifle," I told them and then I began talking about safety. Like where the safety was on the rifle, how to hold the rifle when not using it, and to always be aware of where the barrel of the rifle was pointing when holding it. Next, I explained how to load it. They watched as I opened the bolt on top, loaded a bullet, and closed the chamber by locking the bolt back in place. Then I showed them the bottom of the rifle and how to load more bullets there. Colt and Creed paid careful attention and asked good questions.

After loading four rounds into my rifle, I showed them how to stand and hold the rifle when firing. "There will be kickback. So make sure you hold it firmly," I instructed as I stared through the scope at one of the cans. "Cover your ears. It's going to be loud."

I didn't know if they did, but I gave them a few seconds to do as I'd asked before I pulled the trigger. The butt of the rifle kicked back into my shoulder at the same time the loud shot echoed in the clearing. The bullet I fired missed the can by a few inches and hit the fallen tree trunk beneath it. "One more," I said as I pulled back the bolt all the way, allowing another bullet to enter the chamber, slid the bolt forward, and locked it back into place. I aimed again and fired. Through my scope, I saw the can go flying.

I lowered the rifle and glanced from Colt to Creed, both of whom were lowering their hands from their ears.

"You hit it," Colt said.

"Are you surprised by that?" I asked.

Colt shook his head, smiling at me. "No, my little ball buster."

I tried and failed not to smile. "Who wants to try next?"

Creed volunteered. I handed him the rifle and I walked him through what to do all over again, step by step. When he was ready to pull the trigger, Colt and I covered our ears. Creed fired the rifle.

He got a tiny smile on his face and he lowered the barrel of the gun. "I missed, but I was close."

"Try again," I told him.

After dinner that evening, Knox and Keelan helped me remove my stitches from my arm at the kitchen island while Creed and Colt went down to the basement to pick a game to play.

As Knox snipped and pulled the last stitch out, I let out a sigh as I took in the three-inch-long, rigid line that went across my upper arm. It was dark pink with ugly yellow bruising around it. "Another scar."

"You're still beautiful," Keelan said as he watched me put my sweater back on.

The twins returned with the game Twister. Knox and Keelan opted out of playing but agreed to help us with flicking the spinner. As the twins moved the coffee table out of the way in the living room, I laid out the mat with the colorful circles on it in the center of the room. I was thankful I had changed into leggings and a baggy sweater with a sports bra underneath after we'd come back from shooting earlier today. Leggings would be a lot easier to bend and twist in than jeans. Colt and Creed had also changed into more comfortable clothes; both were wearing long-sleeved shirts with gray sweatpants that left so little to the imagination, they should have been illegal.

When we were ready, Keelan spun the spinner for us. "Right foot on red."

Colt, Creed, and I all stepped on a red circle.

"Before you spin again," Creed said. "I think we should make this game more interesting."

Colt agreed right away.

I folded my arms over my chest. "Here comes the gambling."

"Come down from that high horse, Shi," Creed said with a smirk. "You enjoy it just as much as we do. Or do you need me to remind you of the last time we played with stakes and what you won?"

I had to think for a second to recall the last time we'd placed bets on something.

"What did you compete for last time?" Knox asked.

Just as Creed grinned, I remembered.

"It's not important!" I rushed to say. My cheeks felt like they were burning, and I tried to move the conversation on. "How do you want to do this?"

"With a reaction like that, I really want to know what you three bet on," Keelan said, grinning.

"We told you already," Creed said to Keelan. "At the mud run. You just didn't believe us."

Keelan frowned as he thought back and when he remembered, his eyes flicked to me. "You really bet sexual favors?"

My shoulders slumped in defeat.

"Who won?" Knox asked.

Colt, Creed, and Keelan all said that I had.

"You let me win," I grumbled at Colt and Creed, both of whom were grinning without shame.

"When are you going to cash that win in, Shi?" Creed asked.

Feeling red all over, I refused to answer him.

"Whose idea was it to bet on sexual favors?" Knox asked.

"Shiloh," Colt and Creed said at the same time.

Everyone stared at me, and I had the urge to run from the room. It was pure stubborn will that kept me where I was.

"What did you win, baby girl?" Keelan asked.

If I chose not to answer, I knew Keelan wouldn't push. It hadn't exactly been a private bet. Ethan and Isabelle had heard us discuss the whole thing at the mud run. If I was brave enough to make a sexual bet, then I should be brave enough to talk about it now. I also didn't want Keelan and Knox to think that I would keep things from them that I would only share with Colt and Creed.

I straightened my shoulders. "I bet that if I won, we would try something new in the bedroom."

Knox and Keelan both looked surprised.

Keelan whistled. "I would have let you win, too."

Knox nodded in agreement.

Men! I faced Colt and Creed. "What are the stakes?"

"If I win," Creed said, "you and I get to try something new tonight."

"Sexually?" I clarified.

He nodded with a downright sinful grin.

I shook my head. "I'm still on my period."

His grin dropped. "You say that like you're not allowed to have sex."

I waved my hand over my pelvis in a circular motion. "This area is out of order. It's under refurbishment. No boyfriends allowed."

Colt and Keelan snorted while Creed just shook his head. Knox smartly didn't react.

"Besides, it's embarrassing." I refused to look at Knox as I spoke. "And...and messy. We had to take a shower after."

"We?!" Colt and Creed repeated at the same time.

I snapped my mouth shut.

Colt and Creed looked at each other before glaring at Keelan.

Keelan grinned back at them, eyes full of laughter. "Wasn't me this time." He turned his head to look at Knox sitting next to him.

Colt and Creed gaped at their oldest brother, utterly shocked. Knox just stared back at them, revealing nothing.

"What did you do to embarrass Shi?" Creed questioned him.

Knox gave Creed a look that screamed, *Seriously?*

I let out a frustrated groan. "He didn't do anything. I'm the one who freaked out."

Colt wrapped an arm around my lower back and pulled me to him. "There was no reason for you to freak out, babe."

"Were you more worried about what Knox was thinking or was it you that was uncomfortable with it?" Keelan asked.

My cheeks were so hot, I felt like they were going to melt right off my face. "Can we please move on and play this game?"

"She was worried about me," Knox said, answering for me.

Creed came up and hugged me from behind, sandwiching me between him and Colt. "I think I can speak for all four of us when I say we love you and if you're naked, we don't care what time of the month it is, we're still going to want to fuck you."

"Creed!" I admonished as I stared at Colt, wide-eyed.

Colt smiled down at me. The glint in his eyes told me he wholeheartedly agreed with what Creed had said.

Creed chuckled as he grasped my shoulders and spun me to face him. "If you don't believe me, I'll happily bend you over right now and prove it to you." Creed leaned close and whispered with a naughty smirk, "And to prove that they don't care, either, I bet my brothers would stay and watch me fuck you."

I felt slightly depraved because of how turned on I got. His dirty words painted a dirty picture in my head and all the butterflies in my stomach flew south.

I must have failed to hide what I was feeling, because the smirk Creed had been giving me faded away and genuine surprise took its place.

"I—" My voice came out a little breathy. Looking away

toward the kitchen, I licked my lips and concentrated on keeping my voice calm. "Can we just play the game now?"

Creed's hand grasped my chin and he gently made me look at him. "What do you want if you win, Shi?"

I thought about it. "If I win, I want my feet rubbed for a half an hour."

"From each of us?" Colt asked.

I nodded.

Creed smiled. "Okay." His attention shifted over my shoulder to Colt and a look passed between them. "What do you want? Or do you want to wait to hear what I'm going to ask for?"

Colt thought about it for a second. "I'll wait."

Creed stared down at me, and he brushed his thumb along my jawline. "If I win, I get to touch you anywhere on your body for however long I want to and I can pick the time and location."

Instantly, I was suspicious. "Touch me with what?"

"My hand," he answered with an innocent expression.

That didn't sound so bad. He had already touched every part of my body and I trusted him. "All right."

"I want the same," Colt said, which made me look back at him. He was grinning at Creed as if they had some sort of secret between them.

"Fine. What do you want from each other?" I asked.

Creed shrugged. "Winner picks the next movie we watch."

Colt nodded. "Deal. Let's get started."

Colt and Creed got back to where they'd been standing with their right foot on red. I looked from one twin to the other, feeling like I'd missed something. Hoping they would have some answers, I glanced at Knox and Keelan. Knox was staring at me with an intense look that I couldn't decipher. Keelan appeared thoroughly entertained. Giving up, I went back to where I'd been standing and put my right foot on a red circle.

"I'm going to need a drink if one of them wins," I thought I heard Knox mumble to Keelan.

"A cold shower would be more helpful," Keelan mumbled back and flicked the spinner. "Left hand on blue."

"Pause!" I said.

"There's no pausing, Shi," Creed said, but I ignored him.

Creed let go of his protest the moment I removed my baggy sweater and tossed it to Knox on the couch. I had a feeling I needed to take this game seriously and a loose sweater would just get in the way.

Creed eyed my sports bra. "If you'd like to take off any more of your clothes, I'm sure more time would be given to you. Right, referee?"

Keelan gave us a serious nod. "I'll allow it."

Colt snorted and Knox appeared to be struggling not to smile.

"Left hand on blue," I repeated what Keelan had announced was our next move and I bent over to place my hand on the blue circle.

As the game continued on and more moves were called out, our positions got more complicated. I ended up in a downward-dog position with my butt in the air and my legs wide apart. My face was right between Colt's legs, who was in a crab-like position. His gray sweatpants were making it very hard not to stare. Creed was in a similar position to me, and he was currently resting his forehead on my left butt cheek.

"I don't want you to bend over in public ever again," Creed grumbled.

"Why?" I asked.

I felt his warm breath through my leggings before I felt his teeth. As he bit me, I pushed up to my tiptoes. "Creed!"

"You bent over is too sexy," he said.

Feeling bratty, I said, "Wouldn't it be sexier if I was naked?"

"It's not nice to tease, Shi," Creed said. "Especially when I have this perfect ass in my face."

"You started it," I shot back. "You've been teasing me since before we started playing."

Keelan snickered and flicked the spinner. "Left foot on green."

"Cheese and rice," I grumbled. I'd have to spread my legs even wider to get my foot on green.

Creed and Colt were taller than me, which meant their legs were longer. They both reached a green circle easily. As I put my foot on green, I put more weight on my arms. It didn't take long for them to begin to shake.

"Left hand on yellow," Keelan called out.

Colt cursed but moved his hand from blue to yellow.

In order to move my hand to yellow, I'd have to lean even farther between Colt's legs. Putting my hand on yellow also forced all my weight on my right hand. I tried to focus on breathing, but it wasn't helping. My arm was going to give out soon.

"Right hand on green," Keelan said.

All three of us let out a sigh of relief. Colt moved his right hand onto green easily. I had the choice of reaching over his thigh or under. Over would put me in a plank position over him. Under would put my face right into his crotch.

If he fell, it wouldn't be so bad, though.

As soon as that thought entered my head, a diabolical plan formed in my head. I reached over his thigh to put my hand on green. On the upside, my boobs were resting on his knee. "You know, Colt, this position is giving me déjà vu of the first time I went down on you."

Colt's eyes went wide as they flicked to me.

"Did she just say—" Creed started to say before I talked over him.

"Don't you remember? It was the middle of the night. I was on my hands and knees, and I licked you from base to tip. Then I licked you again before taking you into my mouth."

The room was silent as I spoke, and unbeknownst to Colt, he was slowly sinking to the ground.

Just a little bit more. "Don't you remember how I took you in until you reached the back of my throat? Then I took you in a little bit more to the point I was gagging on your cock. I sucked on your cock like that over and over until I let you fuck my mouth."

Colt's butt hit the ground and he seemed too shocked to realize.

I gave him a sweet smile. "Looks like you lose."

My words took a second to register with him. He finally looked down and didn't seem like he believed it.

Keelan and Knox exploded laughing.

"That was cheating, Shi," Creed grumbled behind me.

"I have no idea what you're talking about," I lied. "I was simply trying to remind him of past events."

"I don't know if I should be mad or proud at what you just did," Colt said as he climbed off the mat and went to go sit on the loveseat across from where Knox and Keelan were sitting on the couch.

"Be proud. She stunned everyone with her filthy little mouth," Keelan said, and he flicked the spinner. "Left foot on blue."

Creed and I continued the game until I was the one in a crab-like position and Creed was in downward dog over the lower half of my body. His face was hovering right over my breasts. Just as he got into that position, he leaned down and nipped the top of my right boob.

"Creed!" I grumbled.

"Isn't that how we're playing now?" he asked me. "Shall I talk about what being in this position reminds me of? Or do you want me to tell you what it makes me think of doing to you right now?"

"Right foot on yellow," Keelan said.

Putting my foot on yellow put strain on my arms again. For Creed, it just seemed to move him closer.

"I liked that look you got on your face earlier," he said.

"What look?" I asked.

"The one you made when I talked about fucking you right here, right now." He ran his lips across the tops of my breasts, making my breath shudder. "Was it the idea of my brothers watching that turned you on?"

I glanced over at Knox and Keelan; both were watching with interest. "Next move, Keelan."

Keelan smiled and flicked the spinner. "Right foot on red."

Crap! I did my best to twist my lower body in that direction and I was just barely able to get my right foot on red. My arms felt like they were going to give out on me at any moment. Creed just had to move his foot over a couple of spaces.

Creed stared down at me with a stupid cocky smirk. "You didn't answer my question."

I glared up at him. "I don't know what you're talking about."

"Right hand on yellow," Keelan said, and I knew I was done for. I couldn't contort my body that way, so I gave up and dropped to the ground.

"Creed's the winner," Keelan announced.

Creed smiled with triumph and lowered himself down to his knees. Not wanting to see him gloat, I rolled onto my stomach and went to crawl away.

Hands grabbed me by my hips and pulled me back until my butt met Creed's pelvis. "Not so fast, Shi."

"What?" I tried to turn to face him, but his hands on my hips firmly kept me on all fours.

"I won," he said as if I needed reminding. "I think I'll claim my prize now."

I stilled as I glanced at Colt, Knox, and Keelan. They watched Creed and me silently. If I knew Creed, the way he intended to touch me was only going to be appropriate for the bedroom. Swallowing, I relaxed. "All right."

Creed slid one of his hands from my hip into the top of my leggings.

"Creed," I said in warning.

"Trust me," he said as his hand slid over my underwear and his fingers found my clit through the thin fabric.

I tried not to react, but my breath hitched, and I rocked backward against his pelvis. His fingers began rubbing that little bundle of nerves, making my hands fist against the mat on the floor. I bit my lip to keep any sounds from leaving me.

"No need to hold back," Creed said. His voice had deepened and with my butt pressed against him, I could feel that he was hard. "I'm not stopping until I make you come."

Feeling the heavy weight of everyone's stares, my cheeks burned.

"Come on, Shi." Creed began rubbing in the way he knew would eventually make me come. "Let us hear those sexy noises."

A whimper escaped as I felt that distinct pressure of release beginning to build. I lowered my forehead to the ground.

Creed's other hand moved from my hip to slide up my stomach and under the bottom of my sports bra. He took one of my breasts in his hand and pinched and tugged on my nipple. The moan that was forced from me filled my ears, filled the room. I felt his cock jerk in his sweatpants at the sound.

"That's it," he encouraged.

I was embarrassed to look at the others. But their silence as they watched tempted me. I glanced at Colt first. He was leaning forward with his elbows resting on his knees. His gaze was fixed on me and the way my body writhed. I looked at Knox and Keelan next. Both were relaxed back on the couch, their eyes slightly hooded as they watched me.

Once that first moan left me, it was like a door had been broken down. As Creed made the pressure build and build between my legs, the more moans slipped past my lips. My body shook. My back arched. My nails dug into the wood floor. I needed something, anything to hold onto to anchor me. As I felt the finish line approaching, I lost control and began rocking my hips.

"Do you want to come, Shi?" Creed asked.

I didn't want to answer.

Creed's fingers stilled.

I smacked the floor. "Yes!"

Creed's fingers started moving again. "Does it turn you on to have us all watch you like this?"

I really didn't want to answer that, but I really, really didn't want him to stop. "Yes," I whispered.

"A little louder," Creed demanded.

I groaned out in both pleasure and frustration. I was right there, right on the edge. "Yes."

The moment the word left me, the pace he was rubbing my clit picked up and I came. Release rippled through me, making my whole body shudder and me cry out, "Yes! Yes! Yes!" It was probably because it was the last word I'd said and coming made my brain short-circuit.

As my orgasm settled, Creed pulled his hands from my clothes and rolled me over onto my back. I didn't resist. My body felt weak and all I could think of doing was breathing. He climbed over me and kissed me. I was so lost in the euphoric aftermath that everything ceased to exist except what I was feeling. I wrapped my arms around him and kissed him back, needing him close, needing all of him.

Right away, I knew he was holding back, and out of desperation, I flipped us so he was sitting with me straddling his lap. I ran my fingers through his hair before tugging on it while I stroked his tongue with mine. His groan rumbled in his chest. The sound fed into my desire, making me crave more to the point I started grinding my extremely sensitive clit against his rock-hard cock.

Creed grabbed my upper arms and poorly tried to pull away. In between kisses he said, "Shi, if we don't stop, I really am going to fuck you."

I wondered why that was a bad thing as I continued to kiss him. Then hands grabbed me under my arms and lifted me up from Creed's waist.

"That's enough for tonight." The sexy, grumbly voice told me it was Knox who'd picked me up. He handed me over to Keelan, who scooped me up like a bride.

"Not cockblocking you, little brother," Keelan shot over his shoulder as he carried me away. "Just trying to prevent any regret she might have later."

Breathing heavily, Creed nodded.

Keelan carried me to my room and set me down near the entrance to the bathroom. "Want to lay down or take a shower?"

Now that I had some distance from Creed, I was a little clearer-headed and I remember my reasons for not wanting to have sex. "I'll take a shower," I said. "Thank you for stopping me."

Keelan gave me an adoring look before he leaned down to kiss me. "Of course, baby girl."

11

THE DAY AFTER OUR GAME OF TWISTER, I TRIED CALLING Logan. It rang once and then my call was sent to voicemail. I took that as a sign that he might be alive. It was disappointing that he hadn't at least called me to see if I was okay, but I guessed he could have checked my GPS tracker and seen that I was here. Instead of wasting his time on me, he was probably busy doing what I had asked him. *Focus on finding him.*

I left him a short message. "As you probably already know, I'm safe. Please call me."

Another three days passed after that, and I checked the burner phone multiple times every day to see if he had called. He hadn't. Not hearing his voice and confirming that he was all right was extremely hard. Not knowing about Isabelle was driving me crazy, too.

The temptation to call her, call Ethan or Ian was so difficult to ignore. But I did it. Every day. To keep us safe, I had to. I tried to tell myself ignorance was bliss. That worked sometimes.

I continued to have nightmares of Mr. X finding us and killing the guys every night. I'd wake up screaming or crying and pissed off. I was tired of it and angry at myself for the helpless part I played in my dreams every time.

It was currently the middle of the night, and I couldn't sleep. It wasn't that I was afraid to sleep like I used to be. Nope. I was too pissed off to sleep. I kept mentally going over what I would have done differently in my previous nightmares if they had been real. It was pointless. Nightmares were not something I could control, but I couldn't help but waste my time fussing over them.

Giving up on sleep, I very quietly and carefully snuck out from between Colt and Creed and off the bed. I thankfully didn't wake them when I left the room.

It was freezing in the living room. It seemed to be the coldest room in the cabin, and we had been using the fireplace every day because of it. The fire we had lit early in the evening was nothing more than cinders now. I added a couple of logs from the stack we kept next to the hearth, and I got another fire going.

At first, I thought I might watch a movie, but my mind was racing too fast to sit still. I ventured into the kitchen. Searching through the pantry cabinet and fridge, I saw that I had all the ingredients I'd need to make homemade baked chocolate doughnuts, which I knew would be a hit with the guys in the morning when they woke up. As I pulled out the ingredients, I noticed bananas on the counter. They were going to go bad soon. I decided to tweak the recipe to make chocolate banana doughnuts instead.

Getting lost in the process of baking was just what I needed. It calmed me and gave me a break from obsessing over useless crap I couldn't control. I didn't have a piping bag, so the doughnuts were going to be a little more rustic-looking than I would have liked, but they would still taste good. After I got the doughnuts in the oven, I cleaned up and prepped to make a chocolate glaze.

When the doughnuts were done, I took them out and set them aside to cool. I was in the middle of making the chocolate glaze at the stove when I heard the wood floor creak behind me. Arms wrapped around my middle before a kiss was placed on top of my head. I knew just from his touch that it was Knox.

"Did you have a nightmare?" His voice came out tired.

"I couldn't sleep." I felt his concern in the way he tensed up a little. Before he could say anything, I spun around to face him and added, "Not because I'm afraid to sleep. My brain wouldn't shut off."

Staring down at me, he brushed a few stray hairs that had fallen from my bun away from my eye. "Do you want to talk about it?"

I shook my head. "I've spent way too much time dwelling on it. I'd rather just bake."

"What are you making?" he asked as he looked around.

I turned back to the stove. "A chocolate glaze to go with the chocolate banana doughnuts I made."

He moved to lean against the side of the island behind me. "Still having chocolate cravings?"

I smiled as I turned off the stove and went to retrieve the now-cooled doughnuts. "No. My period ended yesterday. So the chocolate cravings aren't as strong. The reason for the chocolate doughnuts is because I bought so many things to bake using chocolate."

He nodded and watched as I carried the doughnuts over to the stove. I felt him come up behind me so he could see me dip one side of a doughnut in the glaze and then set it aside to dry.

After I finished dipping a few more doughnuts, Knox startled me a little by grabbing my hand. It was the hand I'd dipped the doughnuts with and my designated hand to get messy with. He pulled my hand up and back a little. I turned my head just in time to see him suck one of my glaze-coated fingers into his mouth.

He let out a deep, rumbly *mmm* as he sucked my finger clean and then moved on to clean the rest that had chocolate on them.

This man had seen me naked. Had done filthy things to my body. But the sound he had just made and the feel of his tongue sliding along my finger...*oh-my-lanta.* That turned me on like a flick of a switch. One second, I was enjoying myself making doughnuts and by the next my body was saying, *What doughnuts?*

"Do I taste good?" I asked with a voice that was slightly high-pitched.

His eyes flicked to mine as he pulled my last chocolaty finger from his mouth. "Every inch of you tastes good."

"I—" I cleared my throat to get control of my voice. "I meant the glaze."

The sinful, knowing smile that graced his face made my heart skip a beat. "No, you didn't," he said.

I pulled my hand from his grasp and stepped out from between him and the stove, needing space.

He frowned at that. "What's wrong?"

"I need to catch my bearings before I embarrass myself," I said.

His frown intensified. "How would you have embarrassed yourself?"

"I almost melted into a horny puddle at your feet," I blurted as I took another step away.

He was quiet for a moment, but his frown disappeared. "And why would you be embarrassed by that?"

"I feel like it should take more than what you did to turn me on."

My response seemed to please him and he flicked his fingers between us. "Come here."

I moved back a little more. I didn't want to just fall into the palm of his hand so easily. Sure, there would be times I'd be inclined to do that, but not today. Maybe I was feeling bratty at the moment or maybe I was in the mood to feel earned. "If you want me, come and take me."

His brows rose slightly before a determined look took over his face. "Are you going to run from me?"

A slow smile stretched across my face. "Maybe."

Before I could finish saying the word, he lunged for me. I took off toward the living room. Arms caught me around my middle just as I reached the couch. Knox spun me around and his hands lifted me up by my butt.

"That was easy," he said as he held me.

"Oh, be quiet," I said just before slamming my mouth over his.

Our kiss started off passionate, but at the first stroke of his tongue, desire began pumping heat through my veins, nearly making me feel crazed.

He carried me a few strides until he was laying me down on the couch. We ripped away each other's clothes in a quick, frantic manner. After we were both naked and Knox retrieved a condom, he knelt between my legs. His large hands ran down my body, starting at my collarbones. Those warm hands paused over my breasts so he could cup them and run his thumbs over my hard nipples. I arched into his touch, wanting more. His pointer fingers joined his thumbs and he tugged and tweaked on the hard buds, making me gasp.

"You're so fucking beautiful," he said as his hands glided down my stomach and around my waist.

Reaching between us, I wrapped my hand around the base of his hard cock. He only let me stroke him twice before he lifted me and arranged us so that I was straddling his lap.

"I want you to ride me," he told me and scooped up the condom from where he'd placed it on the arm of the couch.

As soon as he ripped it open, I took it from him. He didn't protest and watched with a sexy smirk on his face as I rolled the condom onto him. That smirk dropped, though, as soon as I put a hand on his muscled chest and lifted up my hips to align him with my entrance.

I sank down on him slowly. His chest expanded beneath my hand as he inhaled and held his breath until he was completely inside of me. He exhaled a curse and grabbed me by my hips as I started to lift. He gripped tighter as I went to sink down on him again. He wanted me to come back down slowly. So I did and he watched as his cock slid deep inside me.

He loosened his hold on my waist and just rested his hands there as I took back control. "Ride my cock until you come, Shiloh."

"What about you?" I asked as I rolled my hips.

His smirk returned and with it a promise that when it was his turn, I'd thoroughly enjoy it. Until then, he'd watch as I used him. I felt like I'd just been asked to perform the naughtiest show of my life.

I was happy to accept that challenge.

I held onto his shoulders as I bounced and ground on him until I relaxed enough around him to switch things up. He wanted a show, I'd give him one where he could see everything.

I arched back, placing my hands on his knees. As I impaled myself on his cock, chasing that delicious feeling that would deliver my release, my boobs bounced. The way he watched me with darkened and hooded eyes was so sexy to see, it helped spur me toward the edge. As if knowing I was so close by the breathy whimpers that were coming out of me, one of his hands slid up from my waist to the back of my neck and his grip tightened on me. He brought me down harder on his cock as he thrust up to meet me. I cried out every time he did it and when I came, my body tightening up, he kept slamming me down on him over and over again, drawing out my orgasm to the point my head fell back.

His hand at the back of my neck pulled me to him and he kissed me between my panting breaths. As I was still recovering, my limbs feeling weak, Knox sat me on the couch. "Flip over, facing the couch," he ordered.

I got on my knees facing the back of the couch. Standing behind me, he grabbed my hips and pushed back inside me. Groaning, I grabbed ahold of the top of the couch.

"Don't let go of the couch. I'm going to take you hard," he warned as he withdrew and slammed back into me.

The force behind his thrusts nearly made me go cross-eyed. "Oh, God!" I moaned.

He chuckled. "If that's what you want to call me."

"I wasn't—" Thrust. "Calling—" Thrust. "You that." My words came out staggered and breathless.

As he continued to pound into me, one of his hands left

my hip and he fisted my hair, tugging it just enough to border the edge of pleasure and pain. "I'm the only one fucking you, Shiloh. If you don't want me to think I'm a god, you better start moaning my name."

The sounds of my moans and us slapping together were undoubtedly reaching every corner of the cabin. I'd be really surprised if my other boyfriends weren't awake and didn't know exactly what we were doing.

Knox let go of my hair and reached his hand around the front of me between my legs. He began rubbing my clit.

Release slammed into me, making me cry out, "Knox!" My upper body collapsed against the back of the couch, panting.

As I just lay there contracting around his cock, his grip on my hip tightened and his thrusts quickened until he slammed into me one last time. "Fuck," he growled as he came.

We stayed still for a minute, just trying to catch our breath. Then Knox eventually pulled out of me and left to go dispose of the condom. I was in the same position when he returned.

"I think you managed to break me," I said as I watched him put his sweatpants back on and scoop his navy T-shirt off the floor.

Smiling, he lifted me to sit upright, put his T-shirt on me, and laid us out on the couch with me on top of him.

I lay my head over his heart and listened to it beat as I watched the fire. "I need to go finish the doughnuts," I said and let out a yawn.

He began running his fingers up and down my spine. "What you need is sleep. Just rest, Shiloh."

"Did you have sex with me just to tire me out?"

"No. I did that for selfish reasons. But if you're able to get a good night's sleep because of it, I'll take the credit."

I snorted. "Just like you took the title of god?"

"You're the one who called me that."

"I did not!"

His chest shook beneath me as he laughed. I couldn't stop myself from smiling. Nor would I have if I'd been able to. It was a wonderful moment—almost perfect. But intrusive thoughts always found a way to sneak into my mind and I found myself questioning how many more wonderful moments we had left. We were in our own bubble here. How long until someone or something tried to pop it?

I fought with all my might to push those thoughts away and just focus on the feel of the man holding me. I focused hard on his fingers rubbing up and down my spine until my eyes became heavy and I drifted off.

12

I WOKE UP ON THE COUCH ALONE. THE FIRE IN THE FIREPLACE was still burning brightly and I could feel its heat. Sitting up, I threw off the throw blanket that had been covering me. "Knox?" I called out as I looked into the kitchen. The lights were on, but it was empty.

As I stood, I realized that I was dressed in my clothes. Not Knox's shirt. I didn't remember getting dressed before I'd fallen asleep. "Knox?" I called again and tried to look down the hall. It was pitch black. I didn't know why, but the darkness scared me and my legs moved me toward the bright kitchen.

Feeling safe in the light, I convinced myself that Knox was in the bathroom and I headed to the fridge for some water. As I walked by the island, a white ceramic cake stand with a glass dome lid caught my eye. Under the clear glass, I could see the chocolate doughnuts I had been working on were glazed and stacked neatly.

For a second, I wondered if Knox had finished glazing the doughnuts for me. Then I glanced down at my clothes and I started to have doubts. Had I dreamt of Knox and me having sex? Had I made the doughnuts and just fallen asleep on the couch?

"Shiloh," a voice called me.

I looked toward the hall, where I could have sworn the voice had come from, and Mr. X stepped out of the darkness. He was holding a knife in his hand. The blade was covered in blood. So were his hands and the front of his jeans, and some was spattered across his face.

Seeing that blood spiked more fear in me than he did. "Whose blood is that?" I asked even though I knew the answer.

"Shi," I heard Creed call for me. His voice sounded like it was coming from my bedroom down the hall behind Mr. X. I had to get to him. He could be hurt.

Hearing Creed, Mr. X glanced over his shoulder.

"No," I said and to my surprise I was able to move. For once, fear did not shackle me and nothing tried to stop me.

Mr. X turned around toward the hall and I began running for him.

"No!" I screamed, and I was almost about to pass the couch to get to the hall when something locked around my waist. I tried to wriggle and thrash against what felt like a restraint across my hips.

"Don't you touch him!" I yelled at Mr. X.

Mr. X didn't even spare a glance back at me as he stepped into the dark hall, disappearing from sight.

"I'm the one you want!" I thrashed harder to get free. When that didn't work, I threw myself forward toward the floor and the restraint slipped down to my thighs as I went down. Before I could face-plant into the wood floor, I caught myself on my hands. The thing holding me came down with *my lower body and I felt a weight on top of my legs. Using my training, I rolled the weight off of me and started to crawl. I made it about a foot away before my calves were grabbed and I was pulled back. I let out an angry, frustrated scream and what was pulling on me stopped, but didn't let go.*

I kicked to get free and dug my nails into the floor as I tried to crawl forward again. What was latched onto my legs moved up my body to my waist. Using all the strength I had, I dragged myself a few inches forward.

"Shi!" I heard Creed call again, but this time there was panic in his voice.

"If you hurt him, I will kill you!" I roared in a way that sounded feral as I made it forward another inch. "I will cut your fucking heart out!"

I was yanked by my waist from the floor and lifted up to sit. My back collided with something hard yet soft just as weight came down on my legs and my arms were squished against my chest.

"Shiloh, it's not real!" a voice yelled right behind me. "Wake up, baby!"

All it took was a blink and I knew I was awake. The sun was up. The hall that Mr. X had disappeared down was no longer dark and Creed was standing in front of it. I looked to the left and saw Colt and Knox standing in the living room. All three of them were wide-eyed and held panicked looks on their faces.

I was on the ground in the same exact spot I had been in my dream. The thing that had been restraining me hadn't been a thing at all, but someone on the ground right behind me. By process of elimination, I knew it was Keelan. His legs were hooked over mine and his arms were wrapped around me in a rear bear hug hold.

I was breathing heavily. Rage and fear were riding on the back of my adrenaline as it still surged through my veins.

"I think she's awake," Knox said.

I did my best to relax in Keelan's hold. "Did I hurt you?" My voice came out calm, but my tone was a different story. It had a sharp edge to it, revealing how mad I was. I didn't think I'd ever been so angry. Since I'd really started buckling down and working with Dr. Bolton on healing, I'd been getting tastes of anger. This was different. What I was feeling now was a six-course meal. The magnitude of it was altering. I had felt a shift in me coming after what had happened to Isabelle. At first, I hadn't understood it, but I did now. I was done being the victim. I was done being afraid. I was truly done.

If Keelan hadn't stopped me, I might have really tried to kill Mr. X in my dream. I had been so angry I might have followed through on my threat and cut his heart out.

The sigh of relief Keelan let out pulled my attention back to him. His legs lifted off of mine and his arms fell away. He then scooped me up and turned me around to sit facing him. "No, you didn't hurt me," he said as his golden-brown eyes bounced all over my face. "Did I hurt you?"

I shook my head.

Keelan nodded and cupped my face. "Good, because you fought hard."

"He was going to kill Creed." My tone was still angry.

He gave me a tight smile. "So it was my brother you

were going to cut X's heart out for." It was obvious that he was trying to lighten the mood.

I didn't have the heart to tell him that he was more than likely dead in my nightmare. Remembering the blood all over Mr. X made me downright murderous.

Keelan's forced smile turned genuine at whatever he saw in my expression. His hands dropped from my cheeks, and he wrapped an arm around me before flipping us. Next thing I knew I was on my back on the floor with Keelan on all fours above me. My legs were bent to frame his. Cold air hit me right between my legs, bringing to my attention that I wasn't dressed like I had been in my nightmare, but was only wearing Knox's shirt.

"I'm flashing everyone my vagina," I deadpanned as I laid my arms out on the cool floor.

"No one in this room is unhappy about that, Shi," Creed said.

Keelan gave me a mischievous grin. "With how loud you were moaning last night, I wouldn't be surprised if Knox took your panties as payment."

Knox didn't correct him. So I didn't, either.

Keelan stroked my cheek with a finger. "Not a single blush."

"I'm too angry to blush."

"I can see that," he said and sighed. "I wonder what I can do to bring back my blushing girlfriend."

I wanted to tell him to not bother. That he was wasting his time. I didn't feel a beginning or ending to what I was feeling. I was lost in the smoke as my rage burned all around me. I had never wanted to kill anyone before. I had wanted Mr. X dead, but I had never reached a point where I wanted to do it myself.

"Do you want to have sex or do you want to spar, baby girl?" Keelan asked, making me realize that I had gotten lost in my thoughts.

"Why are those my only options?" I asked.

He stroked my cheek again. "Because you need an outlet for that anger."

I debated, but I quickly realized that there wasn't anything to debate. I without a doubt did not want to spar with Keelan when I was angry. I didn't want to risk testing my anger like that. Not with him.

Mind made up, I shifted underneath him and rolled us. He let me pin him on his back without resistance and just grinned up at me. I leaned down and gave him a quick kiss before climbing to my feet. "I want to take a shower," I said as I started walking toward the hall.

Creed had moved into the living room and was sitting on the loveseat. Knox was standing by the couch we had been sleeping on and Colt was standing by the fireplace. They watched me as I approached the hall.

Before I walked down it, I turned and looked back at Keelan, who was still on the floor looking flabbergasted. "Aren't you coming?" I asked him.

Keelan had always been the quickest to process and recover from things and right now wasn't any different. He shot to his feet and rushed to me, but paused as he was about to pass Knox. Keelan stared across the couch at him. "Last night put me in a competitive mood."

"You're not the only one," Creed grumbled as Colt sighed and took a seat next to his twin.

"I love you, brother, but I can't let you outdo me," Keelan said in a way that seemed lighthearted, yet held a hint of seriousness.

Knox folded his arms over his bare chest and the corner of his mouth twitched as he stared back at Keelan. "Good luck."

Keelan gave him a downright feral grin before coming to me. He grabbed my hand and pulled me to my bedroom. I noticed a determined look on his face as he shut the bedroom door and took me into the bathroom. It seemed my jokester of a boyfriend was gone.

He let go of my hand to turn on the shower and I leaned against the sink. "I don't know if I should be upset or not that you two are competing over sex with me."

His back was to me, but I still heard him huff a laugh. He reached behind his head and pulled his shirt off, revealing all his pretty tattoos. When he turned to face me, that determined expression was gone and a sexy smirk had taken its place. He erased the space between us and set his hands on the edge of the sink on either side of my hips, caging me. "We're competing at who can love you better."

"You mean who can fuck me better," I corrected.

"It really is the same thing because competition or not, we love you," he said and frowned a little. "You do realize you'll be benefiting the most from all of this, right?"

I arched a brow. "That's why I don't know if I should be upset."

That made him laugh and he dropped his hands from the sink. He grabbed the end of Knox's shirt and tilted his head toward the now-steaming shower. "Let's get in."

I lifted my arms above my head so he could remove the shirt. I climbed into the shower first while he removed the rest of his clothes. The warm water relaxed me a little. As soon as Keelan got in, his only focus was washing me. He shampooed and conditioned my awful pink hair. He took his time massaging my scalp while he did it. As he washed my body, he rubbed soapy fingers into the tight muscles in my back, shoulders, and legs.

"It's okay to be angry," he said as he was kneeling in front of me, kneading the back of my calf. "You have every right to be and it's normal to feel this way given what you've been through."

"This feels like more than a stage of grief," I said.

He stood up and stared down at me with a serious expression. "Maybe it is more. But anger is anger. You may feel stronger because of it, but it's a hard emotion to control. Anger can make you do and say things you will regret."

I knew that. I just didn't understand why he was telling me. Taking over the washing, I poured some shampoo in my hand and pushed up on my tiptoes to wash his hair. "Are you worried I'll hurt any of you out of anger?"

He wrapped his arms around my waist and pulled me against his naked chest. "No. I just..." He let out a sigh. "Logan is angry and that rage he's carrying around is fueling his need for revenge."

"You think I'm going to run off and go seek revenge on Mr. X?"

"I think if I had not stopped you, you would have tried to kill X in your nightmare."

I didn't deny it. That had been my intention. "Why did you stop me?"

"Because I was scared you'd run into the furniture and hurt yourself," he said as he let me go to rinse out his hair.

I began washing his body after soaping up a washcloth. "I don't have the desire to go out and hunt down Mr. X like my uncle," I said as I ran the cloth over his tattooed skin. "But if he showed up here and he tried to hurt any of you..."

I hated even thinking about it, let alone talking about it. "I've already tried to kill him once. I'll try again. The only change I'll make next time is I'll aim my gun a little higher."

"Hopefully there won't be a next time."

"I hope that, too." Instead of using the washcloth, I used my soapy hand to clean his already-hard cock. I wrapped my hand around his base and stroked down to his tip.

He let out a hiss and stared down between us. I dropped the washcloth and used my other hand to cup his balls as I continued to stroke him.

He put his hand on the wall and he leaned back into the water so the soap would wash away from his body. "Does this mean you're not angry anymore?"

"I'm absolutely pissed." I gave him a firm stroke, making his breath hitch and his hips jut forward, seeking more. "But I'm not pissed at you," I added and dropped to my knees. I ran my tongue along the underside of his cock before sucking him into my mouth.

He let out a curse and his hand went to the back of my head. "I love this side of you."

I released him just long enough to ask, "What side would that be?" And then I slid him back into my mouth to take him in as far as I could.

His head lolled back as he let out a breathy grunt. "I love all of you, but when you bring out this naughty minx side of yours—ah—fuck!"

I made him stumble on his words as I took him deep again. His fingers fisted my hair, and he rocked his hips back and forth, pumping his cock in and out of my mouth, kissing the back of my throat each time.

"You do that so well," he praised with one last thrust into my mouth before reaching down and picking me up.

He lifted me completely off the ground and I locked my legs around his waist. I gasped as he leaned my back against the cool shower wall. He took advantage of my open mouth and slammed his over my lips, his tongue plunging past them to dance with mine. Holding me up with one arm, he slid his other hand between us as he devoured my mouth. I moaned when he found my clit and began rubbing slow firm circles over it.

"When you act like this," he said against my lips as he moved his fingers to my core. "I feel like I can do all the dirty things I've only fantasized about doing to you." He pushed two fingers inside me and began pumping them.

I gripped his shoulders with both hands and tilted my head back against the wall, grunting. "You know I don't like it when you hold back."

He let out a deep, sensual chuckle. "Don't look at it as me holding back." His thumb began rubbing my clit while his fingers fucked me. "Look at it as me enjoying the journey of you becoming ready to accept all of me."

"I've told you before." I hissed and my hips bucked at the sensation of my orgasm building. "I can take you, pretty boy."

The side of his mouth lifted as he curled his fingers inside of me, hitting the perfect spot to detonate my release. "I know you can, baby girl."

I screamed out as I pushed on his shoulders and squeezed my legs around his waist. My body warred with itself, wanting to get away from him while also wanting to keep him close as I came undone.

I watched with hooded eyes as he pulled his fingers from me and put them into his mouth. He made a *mmm* sound. "I think I'm going to need a better taste than that."

He lifted me away from the wall and continued to hold me with one arm as he shut off the shower. When he climbed out with me, he didn't bother grabbing a towel as he carried me into the bedroom and laid me across the foot of the bed. Dripping wet, he climbed on top of me and flipped us so smoothly, it showed off his years of martial-arts training. Grabbing me by my waist, he pulled me up his body. "I want you to sit on my face."

I crawled up him and set my knees on either side of his head and began to lower myself down. We had done this position once before, but that time I'd had the headboard to help me hover over him. This time, with where we were lying on the bed, I did not.

I lowered myself just enough to bring myself to his mouth. His tongue swiped out, licking through the pool of wetness my release had made. He slipped that tongue inside me before moving it between the folds of my pussy to my clit. It felt so good, my thighs began to shake as I fought the desire to sit and grind on his face.

As if sensing my need, Keelan's hands tried to pull me down by my hips. "I told you to sit," he said from between my legs.

Had this been at any other time and had I been in a more patient mood, I would have resisted out of fear. But because I was in a *to hell with it* mood, I gave him what he asked for. I sat. He began sucking and licking my clit as if rewarding me for doing as I'd been told.

I decided it was best to let go at that point and just give in to my body and its desires completely. I leaned forward to set my hands on the bed and began moving my hips in sync with his tongue.

Cheese and rice. The noises that came out of me should have been embarrassing. But I didn't have it in me to care.

As I felt myself reaching release, I moved a hand to the top of Keelan's head and fisted his soft blond hair. I came so hard, my vision went spotty. My entire body shook and became limp as Keelan flipped us once again.

Lying on my back, panting, I watched as he licked the corner of his mouth and wiped his wet chin with the back of his hand. "I can't decide if I want to fuck you or have you ride my mouth again."

All I could do was groan and throw my arm over my eyes.

He huffed a laugh. "You make the sexiest noises when you grind that little clit against my tongue." The bed shook beneath me—he was moving around. Then I heard the sound of the nightstand drawer opening, followed by the distinct sound of a foil packet being ripped open.

I had just caught my breath when he grabbed me by the backs of my knees and dragged me across the bed until my butt reached the edge. I threw my arm off my eyes to see that he was standing on the floor. He placed my ankles on his shoulders before he pushed his cock inside of me.

I was so sensitive from coming twice already. "Fuck, Keelan!"

He chuckled. "That's what I plan on doing." He pumped his cock inside me a few times before he moved his hands to the backs of my knees and pushed my thighs to my chest. He held them there as he watched his cock go in and out of me slowly. The groan of pleasure he let out at what he saw made me clench around him. His thrusts picked up the pace until he was pounding into me.

I was still so sensitive that the pleasure was almost too much to bear. "Please!" I begged, but I didn't know if it was for him to stop or to keep going. When I was on the cusp of coming, tears began to leak from the corners of my eyes. "Keelan!"

Because he was holding me down, all I could do was fist the blankets beneath me as I was completely wracked by another orgasm. I lost hearing for a short time. I lost sight, too. Well, I closed my eyes, but my point was that I was so consumed with feeling what he'd unleashed on me that I almost missed his climax.

His thrusts started to sputter until he slammed into me one last time, grunting. He wobbled a little and let out a curse as he let go of one of my legs to catch himself on the bed.

"What's wrong?" I asked.

He laughed in between pants. "You're the only woman who has ever made me go weak in the knees."

I laughed as I wiped away the streaks of tears next to my eyes.

He went still. "Those are good tears, right?"

I smiled at him. "I came so hard it made me cry. So I would say yes, they are good tears."

Keelan smiled back at me. Pushing my legs apart, he leaned between them to give me a kiss. Then another one, before pulling out of me and going back into the bathroom to dispose of the condom.

I took that time to scoot farther back on the bed. When he returned, he crawled onto the bed next to me and laced his fingers behind his head. "Still feeling angry?"

I snorted. "I don't think it's possible to still be angry after three orgasms."

"It shouldn't be possible to be angry after one orgasm,

but you were ready to commit murder. I figured I would play it safe and give you three."

I reached for a pillow and smacked him with it, making him laugh as he blocked it with his arm. "Don't act like you were doing me any favors. You were only trying to show up Knox," I said and smacked him with the pillow again.

He snatched the pillow away with a chuckle. "I'll be honest, baby girl, I forgot all about my brother the moment you dropped to your knees in the shower." He tossed the pillow to the side and lunged for me.

I fought to prevent him from pinning me. It was odd and kind of a turn-on, despite just having had sex, to somewhat spar while naked. Both of those feelings distracted me enough to give him the upper hand. I wound up on my stomach with his hands pinning mine behind my back and his cock nestled between my butt cheeks. I bucked up against him in a futile attempt to get him off of me. All it did was make him grow hard again. I guessed I wasn't the only one getting turned on sparring naked.

He let out a breathy laugh. "That first time you grounded me, I really thought I might have met my soulmate." His lips pressed to my spine, making me squirm. I tried to pull my wrists from his grasp as he started trailing kisses up. "I am certain now that you are," he added.

His words made me stop resisting. "I love you, pretty boy."

I felt his mouth stretch into a smile between my shoulder blades. "I love you, too, baby girl."

When his kisses reached my neck, I tilted my head to the side to give him better access.

"I don't think we'll be leaving this room today," he whispered in my ear.

13

LATER THAT NIGHT, WE WERE ALL SITTING IN THE LIVING room. I was lounging on the couch getting my feet rubbed by Colt while Creed, Knox, and Keelan were sitting on the floor around the coffee table playing cards. We had a fire going and I found myself in a trance watching the flames as I ran my finger over the long scar that went up my inner arm.

"What are you thinking about, babe?" Colt asked.

I blinked a few times to break free. "I was thinking about how I got this scar."

Knox, Keelan, and Creed went silent.

Colt's hands stilled on my feet. "What made you think of that?"

"My hair," I answered. It had been over a week and I still wasn't used to it. I still saw her when I looked in the mirror. "I had built these walls inside my head to help keep that night buried in the furthest corner of my mind. I've been working to tear those walls down to face what happened that night. That day Logan showed you the pictures of all of Mr. X's victims, I only told you what I could about the night my family was murdered because that was as far as I could get before I hit a wall."

Creed, Knox, and Keelan had frozen in the middle of their game. None of them were looking at the hand of cards they each held. Instead, their focus was on me.

"It was the last wall and I thought it was going to be the hardest one I'd have to tear down. I don't know exactly when it happened, but I discovered the wall wasn't there anymore when I was getting stitched up at Micah's shop."

"I was surprised when Alaric asked you about your scars and you were so forthcoming on how you got them," Colt said.

"I think that wall went down because I needed it to," I said, and then let out a humorless huff of a laugh. "Which really shows how hard I've been making this whole facing-my-past crap for myself."

"Why did you need the wall to go down?" Knox asked.

I met his eyes. "Because I needed to be able to look back at that night and learn anything I could from it, so I won't make the same mistakes again." I took my feet off of Colt's lap and put them on the floor. Resting my elbows on my knees, I ran my finger over my scar again. "Keeping us safe is more important than my fear of the past."

Knox put his cards on the table and got up to sit on the loveseat across the room on the other side of the coffee table. He locked his eyes with mine. "How did you get that scar?"

My finger stilled over the middle of it. Taking a second, I emotionally prepared myself for what I was about to do. I knew it was time and the best part was that I was finally ready to tell them. "If I'm going to tell you that, I should probably start from where I left off."

"You were hiding in your father's office with Shayla," Colt said.

I nodded.

⁓

That Night

Part 2

When Shayla opened the door, light from the TV in the living room poured into the dark office. Very slowly, she peeked out.

"It's clear," she whispered and took my hand.

I followed her out. She squeezed my hand as we passed our dad on the couch. Tears silently rolled down my cheeks and off my chin when we had to step over our mom's body.

We were headed for the front door. As soon as it was in sight, I noticed that the foyer light was on. If Shayla noticed, she didn't seem to care. She began to walk faster.

As soon as we stepped into the bright foyer, Mr. X stepped out of our mom's darkened office directly across the room from us. Seeing him, Shayla stopped in her tracks so suddenly that I ran into her.

A terrifying smile stretched across his face as his eyes landed on me. "There you are."

With where he was standing, there was no way we'd get to the door without him catching us.

Coming to a decision before I could, Shayla yanked me toward the stairs, which were just to our left. We climbed up as fast as we could and just as we reached the top, I glanced back to see Mr. X taking his time coming up the stairs behind us.

The upstairs hall light was on. It had been off when I'd gotten home.

Shayla didn't let go of my hand as she ran ahead of me down the hall. We passed her room. Then mine. The lights in our rooms were off. She led us into our parents' room and let go of my hand just as we got inside. One of the lamps on our parents' nightstands was on. Why did I feel like we'd been led here with light?

Shayla slammed the door closed, but it bounced open. "Oh my God," she gasped when she reached for the door-knob and there wasn't one. Just an open hole where it should have been.

I looked around for any idea of what to do and ran to our parents' dresser. "Help me."

Using all the strength I had, I started pushing the heavy wooden dresser toward the door. Shayla quickly joined me, and we both got the dresser up against the door.

Shayla pointed across the room. "The window."

We both rushed to it. Shayla got there before me and pushed it open. We eyed the far, straight drop to the ground. "We can make it," she said and started to put her legs out the window.

I grabbed her arm. "No, we won't. That drop guarantees broken bones and we won't get far if we can't walk."

"We'll try to lower ourselves down as far as we can before we drop," Shayla said frantically.

"Oooh, Shiii…loooh," Mr. X sang from just outside the bedroom door.

"There's no time," I whispered.

Shayla stared out the window, torn, before nodding.

"Hide," she mouthed. She brought her leg back in and pulled me to the bed. "Get under here."

I dropped to the floor and quickly crawled under the bed. When I was halfway under, Mr. X started shoving against the door. Shayla rushed to our parents' closet. Just as I was fully hiding under the bed, Mr. X got the door open enough to squeeze sideways into the room.

All I could see were his boots. I held my breath as I watched those boots stand near the door for a moment and then slowly make their way over to the window we'd left open.

I did my best not to make a sound while silently hoping that he'd think we'd taken the risk of escaping through the window. He paused by the window for a few seconds before walking back toward the door. For a painful, pounding heartbeat, I thought he was going to leave the room, and then he rounded the bed and headed for the closet.

Shayla!

Moving as quietly as I could, I started scooting out from the opposite side of the bed, still watching Mr. X stand facing the closet. I was almost completely out from under the bed when he turned on the light in the walk-in closet and moved farther inside. I heard the rustling of hanging clothes being shoved to the side as I slowly sat up and peeked over the top of the bed at the closet.

Shayla let out a scream full of terror, making me jump into action. I leapt onto the bed and crawled across it quickly. Before I reached the other side, I spotted the unlit lamp on my dad's nightstand. I grabbed it and yanked the cord from the wall as I came up behind Mr. X, who was dragging Shayla out from the corner of the closet where she'd been hiding.

Using all my strength, I swung the vase-shaped lamp at his head. The ceramic body of the lamp shattered against his skull and Mr. X let out a grunt before dropping to his knees. He loosened his grip on Shayla's pink hair enough for her to get herself free and leap off the ground.

We both rushed out of the closet and toward the door. Mr. X had only scooted the dresser far enough to squeeze past it. Opening the door until it met the dresser, I slipped out of the room first. I only glanced back to make sure Shayla was right behind me. She was in the process of coming out of our parents' room. I didn't see Mr. X behind her. A little bit of relief flickered inside me, and I ran down the hall with my hand held out behind me for Shayla to take.

She never took it.

I passed my room and was almost about to pass hers when I heard her yelp. Stopping, I spun around, and my heart tried to lodge itself in my throat. Mr. X had her in his grasp. Her back was to his chest. He held her to him with an arm around her middle and his knife pressed so firmly to her throat, she was tilting her head back as if to get away from it.

"Please," I begged with my hands out in front of me.

"Please what, my Shiloh?" he asked. There was such disgusting delight in his voice. It was as if this was all a game to him.

I took a tiny step forward. "Please don't hurt her."

Mr. X threw his head back laughing. "Oh, my darling, are you sure you want that? After all, she's why I came for you."

What?

"Shi," Shayla whimpered, and tears started falling from her eyes.

Mr. X pressed his knife into her delicate skin a little

more and a line of blood slid down her neck and over her collarbone.

"How do you think I knew they were going to take you from me?" he asked and stared down at Shayla. "Your sister here is the one who told me."

"No," Shayla forced out.

He leaned his mouth close to Shayla's ear. "Don't remember? You were in that cafe you love to go to with your friends. All you did was whine and complain to them about your pathetic spoiled life." A smile stretched slowly across his face. "I was sitting at the table behind you listening. I was hoping to hear about how your father reacted to the video I sent him the day before, but you revealed so much more."

All the blood in Shayla's face seemed to drain and her wide eyes flicked to me.

Mr. X's eyes rolled to me, too. "I don't know why she is so precious to you. She is nothing more than a toxic tether holding you back from me, and I will cut you free from her."

My sister's brows scrunched together and something flickered in her eyes. Acceptance, maybe? Because in that moment, we both knew what was going to happen. She had accepted it—accepted that she was about to die, and she had done it so quickly while I stood there frozen, terrified, and unwilling to accept it.

"Shi, run!" she cried out just before Mr. X slid his knife across her throat, silencing her forever.

Blood poured like a crimson waterfall from her neck. Her gray eyes were wide, filled with terror as they held mine.

I couldn't move.

I couldn't look away.

I didn't want to believe what I was seeing was real. It wasn't real. It couldn't be. I was certain that if I could close my eyes, what I was seeing would be undone.

With each passing second, I watched the spark of life within her eyes dim. My shared soul, the person who'd come into this world with me, was being ripped away. Disbelief was quickly yielding to the sharp power of truth and there wasn't anything I could do to stop it.

Mr. X unhooked his strong arm from around Shayla's middle and shoved her forward. Without resistance she fell, crumpling to the floor in the hallway right in front of my bedroom. Blood pooled around her, seeping into the beige carpet, staining the ends of her cotton candy pink hair a bright red.

My heart raced at a painful rate, booming in my ears with a rapid *thump! thump! thump!*

I should have run like Shayla had told me, but I wasn't in my body. My soul had left me, and it was standing next to her, begging for any sign that she was still alive.

Please move!

Her fingers twitched on the blood-soaked carpet and hope bloomed in my chest. My gaze tore away from her to Mr. X. His booted foot took an ominous, slow step over her body while his monstrous coal eyes held mine. There was blood splattered across his face, clashing against his alabaster skin. An evil smile pulled at the corners of his mouth as he took another step, then another, closing the distance between us.

I knew I needed to run, but I couldn't feel my legs.

"*Shiloh,*" he sang my name. His voice was light yet haunting and made my entire body tremble.

Move!

Move!

If you don't, you won't be able to get help for Shayla!

The need to save my sister overshadowed my terror by a hair, but it was just enough to give me back my ability to move.

When I was almost within Mr. X's reach, I spun on my heels and ran for the stairs. He didn't take his time coming after me like he had when Shayla and I had run up the stairs. I could hear his boots pounding behind me, shaking the pictures on the hall wall.

My own feet raced down the stairs as I'd done so many times before when running late for school. I made it halfway down when Mr. X caught me by my shoulder and shoved me against the wall.

I tried to fight him by pushing and smacking him. He easily caught both of my wrists and pinned them high above my head with one hand. In the process, we knocked one of my family's portraits off the wall and the glass broke as it tumbled down the stairs.

He pressed his body into mine. "Why do you love to run from me?" He leaned his head forward as if to kiss me and I quickly turned my face to the side. His mouth touched my cheek, and he ran his tongue along it until he reached my ear. "We are free to be together now."

"I don't want to be together!" I snarled.

He leaned back with an unhappy frown. "Yes, you do. We love each other."

I shook my head. "No!"

"Yes," he growled, clearly getting angry. "You are mine."

"No! I'm not yours!" I cried.

He roared angrily in my face before he brought up his

knife and placed the tip to my inner wrist. "Yes, you are." He began carving something into my skin.

The pain made me scream and I thrashed. I got the bottom of my foot pressed against the wall to help propel me forward at the same time I flung my head toward his face. My forehead smacked his chin hard. It made him grunt and shocked him enough for me to push off the wall with my foot and shove him back.

What I hadn't planned on was his knife slicing down my arm from my wrist to my elbow as he fell backward. The pain made me scream. It was quickly cut off when Mr. X's back hit the banister and he jerked in pain, which caused him to push me away from him. I felt myself falling and, in an attempt to save myself, I grabbed his shirt. Because he wasn't aware I had done that, he wasn't able to brace for it. I took him down the stairs with me.

The wind was knocked from my lungs as I landed on my butt and ribs. My feet flung in the air as I flipped and I braced for what would surely break my neck, but as I came down again, I landed on top of Mr. X. He let out a loud exhale, as if all the air was forced out of his body. The both of us slid the rest of the way down and rolled along the floor. Mr. X didn't stop rolling until he slammed into the front door. His body stopped me.

It took longer than it should have to remember how to breathe. When I was able to snap out of the shock, I gasped loudly, taking in the air that I desperately needed, and rolled over onto my stomach.

I need to get up.

My body hurt so badly that I struggled to do more than lie there and breathe.

Get up!

Mr. X groaned next to me. The fear that noise conjured sent a new surge of adrenaline through me. I made myself get on my hands and knees. Just to put distance between me and him, I crawled until I felt strong enough to push up to my feet.

I stumbled, falling against the hall wall as I passed the stairs, heading toward the back of the house. Blood from my arm smeared against the wall, reminding me that Mr. X had cut me.

I picked up my pace as I headed past the entrance to the kitchen and entered the mudroom that led to the door to the garage. I didn't dare turn on any lights. Mr. X would come looking for me soon. Lighting up where I was in the house would only get me found faster.

Going right to the door that led to the garage, I turned the handle and went to pull it open. It wouldn't. I could see that it was unlocked; the handle wouldn't have been able to turn otherwise. I pulled on the door a few more times as I looked up and saw why it wouldn't budge. At least ten nails were hammered along the top of it.

Not wanting to waste a moment, I went into the laundry room just off of the mudroom. There was a window in there that faced the side yard. I rushed to it. After unlocking it, I tried to push it open. It didn't budge. I searched the sill and found that it was also nailed shut.

The doorknob in our parents' room was gone and now I was finding a window and door nailed shut. Mr. X had turned my house into a trap.

Not wanting to give up, I moved on. My inner arm was bleeding a lot. Blood dripped from my fingers as my arm dangled at my side limply, leaving a bloody trail in my wake as I quietly snuck through the house.

"Shiiiii…loooooohh! Come out, come out, wherever you are!" Mr. X shouted from another room.

Dashing into the kitchen, I scooped up one of the kitchen towels hanging in front of the oven. Biting my lip to keep myself from crying out, I wrapped the towel around my arm. I made quick work of my makeshift bandage and kept moving. I couldn't linger or he'd find me.

Walking as silently as possible, I headed for the back door just off the dining room. Reaching out for the gold doorknob, I turned it. The door wouldn't budge. "No!" I whispered as I vainly tried to slam my body against it.

The feeling of being trapped made it hard to think of what to do.

"Shiloh," a voice whispered from behind me.

My heart accelerated to a speed so fast, I was afraid it'd give out. Panting, I turned to find Mr. X right behind me. I screamed as loud as my lungs would allow, hoping the neighbors would hear, and fell backward to the floor.

Mr. X dove with me, landing on top of me. I tried to fight him. I tried to get away. I was able to smack him across the face, which angered him. He let out a snarl, covered my face with his hand, and slammed the back of my head to the tile floor.

My vision went in and out. I didn't feel myself being lifted off the floor or carried through the house. I started to really come to as Mr. X was carrying me up the stairs. We were almost back on the second floor. I started to wiggle and buck in his arms as he reached the top of the stairs, so much so that he ended up dropping me with a frustrated growl.

I hit the carpet with a grunt. Before I could attempt to get away, Mr. X grabbed my ankles and began dragging me down the hall. I grabbed ahold of the corner of the wall trying to stop him. Mr. X yanked with what seemed like all his strength to force me to let go. My nails tore into the wallpaper as he continued dragging me. The towel I had wrapped around my arm fell off. I let out another pain-riddled scream, despite knowing that no one could hear me. That knowledge had been proven when our neighbors hadn't come running to my earlier screams. Our houses were just too far apart.

I tried to kick my legs free, but Mr. X's grip was too strong, and his steps didn't slow. I was so focused on trying to grab ahold of anything that came into reach that I didn't realize we were passing Shayla's body until I felt something wet seep into the back of my clothes. At the sight of her pink hair, my throat closed, and I began choking on my sobs. I grabbed her hand as it came into reach, desperately hoping to find some flicker of life still left in her. When our eyes were level with each other, I saw hers were open and vacant.

"No!" ripped out of me. "Shayla!" I wailed, squeezing her hand as Mr. X continued to pull me away from her and into my bedroom.

As soon as we were in my room, Mr. X pulled me off the floor by my hair. My throat was so sore from screaming, all I could do was grit my teeth through the pain. He was trying to get me on my bed. I couldn't let him do that. He'd rape me. I just knew he would.

The moment my feet were flat on the ground, I hit him, kicked him, and scratched him. He grunted a curse when I clawed his cheek.

His hand wrapped around my throat and squeezed. Digging my nails into his hand and wrist that held me, I tried to suck in what little air I could. His other hand appeared out of nowhere. I only got a glimpse of it before pain flared like lightning on the left side of my face and everything went black.

When I came to, I was alone and lying in the center of my bed. I went to rub my sore cheek and found that my wrist was caught on something. That was when I realized my wrists were tied with rope to my bed posts. As I tried to sit up, I realized my ankles were tied up as well.

Panic made my chest cave in, and I cried. Everything that had happened came crashing down on me. My parents were dead. Shayla...my lip trembled as I remembered her lifeless eyes.

I was alone.

I was all alone.

14

THAT NIGHT

IT WOULD HAVE BEEN SO EASY TO JUST GIVE UP—TO JUST let him have me.

Bury it, Shiloh. Shayla's voice filled my head.

I closed my flooded eyes. Tears spilled from them. Two chest-shaking, silent sobs escaped before I was able to take a deep breath. "Okay," I whispered. I took another deep breath, and with that breath, I found the strength I needed to push back the pain and heartbreak.

"Okay," I whispered to myself again and opened my eyes.

I shifted, scooted, and pushed with my heels to help me sit up against the headboard. The rope around my ankles went taut when I was about halfway to sitting all the way up. At least I wasn't flat on my back, and I could see the door.

I tried tugging on the rope on my right wrist to test its strength. It was pretty strong. Mr. X was determined I wouldn't escape. But I could twist my wrist within the rope tied around it. I tried to twist and pull to see if I could squeeze my hand out. It didn't work. If only I could stretch out or wear down the rope somehow, I might be able to get free.

With that plan, I started twisting and pulling at all of my bindings, never removing my eyes from the door.

Twist. Twist. Pull.

That was the only thing that mattered. If I wanted to survive—to get free—it was all that could. The only thing that kept me company for what felt like hours was my fear.

At some point, blood slowly started to roll up my arms toward my elbows. My pillows were stained with dark red dots and down by the foot of the bed, beneath my ankles, were large copper blotches that had seeped into my gray comforter. The tan ropes tied around each of my wrists and ankles looked as if they had been dipped in red wine.

Twist. Twist. Pull.

I'd repeated that process over and over again—rubbing away my skin against the splintering rope as I did.

How long had it been since Mr. X had tied me to my bed and left me? He had brought me in here when it had still been dark outside. The sun was up now. It had been up for a while.

My eyes were glued to my open bedroom door, feeling as though Mr. X would appear at any moment. I tried not to let my eyes drift to the tips of Shayla's white sneakers. He had slit her throat just outside my bedroom. Her body was still where she'd fallen. She was dead. There was no denying it now. I had tried to get help—tried to escape. But Mr. X had nailed the windows and doors. The only door I hadn't tried was the front door. Mr. X had caught me before I could.

I had a feeling that was the only way out.

Twist. Twist. Pull.

Strangely, the pain of my nerves rubbing against the rope

had numbed. Was it my need to escape—my adrenaline blocking out the one thing that could slow me down?

It didn't matter. I didn't need to know. I had no idea when Mr. X would come back. I wouldn't let myself think about what he would do to me when he did. I just had to get out of here.

Twist. Twist. Pull.

The rope around my right wrist slid up around my hand. I held my breath as I pulled on it again and the rope squeezed over the rest of my hand, passed over my fingers, and I was free. A new surge of hope and relief rushed through me.

"Oh, Shiii…loooh!" Mr. X sang, his voice echoing from down the hall. I was so tired of him calling for me that way. There was no doubt that sound would haunt me for the rest of my life if I survived this.

He began humming as he made his way down the hall toward my room. I worked quickly to untie my other wrist as I listened to him getting closer. Once my other hand was free, I glanced down at my tied ankles. I wouldn't be able to untie them in time. Panicked, I searched around. There was a pen on my nightstand. I reached for it. My fingers were barely able to roll it close enough to scoop it into my hand.

Moving as fast as I could, I wrapped the rope back around each wrist, praying that he wouldn't notice that they weren't tied. I hid the pen in my clenched fist behind the taut rope. My gaze went back to the doorway just in time to see Shayla's feet slide away.

My hand that wasn't holding the pen squeezed around the rope so tightly it was painful. I needed that pain. I needed it to be worse than the fear that was threatening to paralyze me.

Mr. X stepped into view. Only he wasn't alone. He was holding Shayla's limp body against him with an arm around her waist and his hand held one of hers. Then he waltzed into my room, quite literally. Still humming, he spun around— dancing with her lifeless body. As he dipped her, he said, "Your sister always was the attention whore." He stood straight and stared down at Shayla, whose head flopped around like a newborn baby's. "Even though you two are identical, you couldn't be more different." He spun around again, swinging Shayla with him. "She flaunted herself about, gobbling up every ounce of attention she got like a greedy, spoiled princess. She may have been beautiful on the outside, but her soul was ugly." He tossed Shayla's body to the ground and his eyes flicked to me. "You, however, are perfection. Inside and out. You don't have to flaunt anything. Your soul radiates a genuine and pure light. It calls to me." He walked over to my bed. Eyes never leaving mine, he brought his knee up onto the mattress. "Your innocence draws me in like a moth to a flame," he said as he crawled over me until he was straddling my hips. His hands cupped my face. "I covet that innocence." His hands moved down and around my neck. "I want it so bad…" He squeezed. "I almost want to destroy it."

He cut off my air completely. Panic flared through me, taking over. I thrashed and bucked beneath him, almost forgetting that my hands were free. I quickly worked to shed the rope.

"You are mine, Shiloh. No one can take you from me now," he growled as he continued to choke me.

I got the rope off my hand holding the pen.

Do it! Do it now! I screamed internally. Fisting the pen in my hand, I swung it. I stabbed the pen through his cheek.

"AH!" he screamed, rolling off of me and off the bed. He hit the ground with a loud thump that shook my room.

I didn't waste any time and started untying the rope around my ankles. I got one untied pretty quickly, then jumped to the next one. He groaned loudly and crawled toward the bathroom connected to my room.

As soon as I had my last ankle untied, I quickly clambered off my bed. I jumped over Shayla's body and ran for the door. I was caught by my foot and fell forward. The moment I hit the ground, I was dragged back.

I started kicking my legs and because my ankles were bloody, his grip on me slipped. He let out a loud roar as I started to crawl away. I pushed to my feet and ran for the door again. By his ragged breathing, I knew he was right behind me. Not wanting a repeat of what had happened on the stairs, I made a last-second decision to turn right, the opposite direction from the stairs, as I ran out of my room. I had a plan in my head, and I prayed it would work.

Pushing my beaten body to the max, I returned to my parents' bedroom door. I squeezed through the door quickly. Just as I got inside, Mr. X tried to grab me. I let out a yelp as I leapt away and dashed for my parents' en suite.

Just like the bedroom door, the doorknob was missing from the bathroom door. I'd anticipated that. My parents' bathroom had a linen hutch for their towels, extra bedding, and other stuff they'd chosen to store in there. I put my back to the side of it, set my feet on the wall, and pushed. Grunting loudly, I used the strength in my legs to knock over the heavy hutch in front of the door just as Mr. X tried to shove it open. The sound of the hutch crashing to the floor echoed loudly in the bathroom, followed by Mr. X yelling my name on the other side of the door.

The hutch wouldn't keep him out for long, which I'd known before coming in here. I rushed across the bathroom over to what looked like a cabinet door in the wall near the shower. It wasn't a cabinet. My parents' bathroom was located over the laundry room. And the door in the wall was a laundry chute.

When we had been kids, Shayla and I used to climb down the chute. I was older and bigger now, but I was certain I could still fit. Ripping open the door, I peered down the narrow tunnel made of wood. It was going to be a tight fit. As soon as I started to slide my body into the chute feet-first, Mr. X started ramming against the door with what I assumed was his whole body. If he kept doing that, he'd get inside in no time.

Moving as fast as I could, I continued lowering myself into the tight tunnel. I put my feet tightly against the walls of the chute to help lower me down and to keep me from falling. As soon as I was fully inside, I closed the door to the chute. Nothing could be seen but darkness. I did my best not to focus on it and started working my way down, trying to be as quiet as possible.

"Shiloh!" Mr. X roared and I froze. His stomps as he moved around the bathroom made the walls in the chute vibrate.

When they started to sound far away, I moved down some more. I was almost to the bottom when the door to the chute was ripped open.

"Shiloh!" he yelled down at me.

I only glanced up at him for a second, to see him staring down at me, before dropping down the chute the rest of the way. I fell into a basket that was sitting on top of the dryer to catch the clothes. Because the basket was too small for my body, it tipped over and I fell to the floor. I tried to catch myself with my hands. They slowed down my fall a little, but the rest of me still smacked to the ground.

Breathing heavily and starting to feel pain, I got to my feet. The first few steps I took, I limped. As I made my way out of the laundry room and into the mudroom, I tried my best to quiet my breathing.

I had two ways to get to the front door. I could go through the guest bathroom to my mom's office or take the hall by the stairs. Stepping out of the mudroom, I turned left and cut through the Jack-and-Jill guest bathroom that led to my mom's office. Taking the hall by the stairs would leave me too exposed.

Before I stepped out into the foyer, I leaned on the wall in my mom's office so I could peek out. I looked up the stairs and down the hall and tried to see into the living room straight across the foyer. I didn't see Mr. X anywhere. Silently, I stepped out of my mom's office. With the front door in my sight, I crept toward it. I strained to listen for any sound that would give me a hint of where Mr. X was in the house. I heard nothing. Just the hum of the air-conditioning blowing through the vents.

Ten more steps until I reached the front door...nine more steps...eight more...

The wood floor creaked under the weight of my foot. My whole body tightened up as the sound echoed through the silent house. With my heart booming in my ears, I took a quick look around, bracing for him to jump out. When he didn't, I zeroed in on the front door. It was my only hope— my only way out. I rushed the remaining distance, my pace quick and no longer quiet. I lifted my hand, reaching for my freedom.

My fingers barely brushed the doorknob when a hand grabbed me by my hair and yanked me back. I let out a loud, broken scream as my back collided with the front of Mr. X's body.

"I can't let you go." His cold voice was devoid of emotion.

That made me pause. In the nick of time, I saw his knife coming up toward my throat. I caught his wrist and forearm with my hands before the knife could reach me.

He pulled my head back harder, exposing my throat. I let out a strangled grunt as I fought against his strength. His knife inched closer and closer as my arms weakened.

Think!

I took the risk of looking around, desperate to find anything that would help me. There was nothing close.

Think! What would Logan do?

I thought back to the few self-defense moves he had taught Shayla and me on our last trip to Texas. We had been at the beach. The memory of Shayla's laughter echoed in my head; she'd pretended to stomp on Logan's instep and dropped to the sand, squealing as she'd crawled away from him. She hadn't taken Logan's lesson seriously but had humored him nonetheless.

I pulled myself back to my horrific reality. With the last bit of strength I had, I pushed Mr. X's blade back a little, then slammed my foot down on his. The moment his grunt reached my ears, I dropped to the floor, losing a good chunk of hair in the process. I refused to let the burning on my scalp slow me down. I shot back to my feet and hurried for the door.

"No!" he bellowed behind me before a searing pain sliced across my shoulder blade. Crying out, I stumbled and fell against the door. I grabbed the doorknob to keep me from falling completely to the ground. I twisted it, the door swung open, and I felt the warmth of the sun on my skin for only a breath before his arms locked around my waist. Lifted into the air, I thrashed and screamed as loud as I could, hoping anyone might hear me with the door open.

Then I was airborne.

The air was knocked from my lungs as my spine slammed against the wooden stairs. Mr. X braced himself above me by holding himself up with one hand on the step behind my head. "You are mine!" he roared in my face. Spittle hit my cheeks and his rancid breath filled my nose.

My breath hitched. Not from the smell. But from the excruciating pain that exploded in my stomach.

He had stabbed me.

His knife was buried in my stomach. Time slowed as he withdrew. His eyes were dilated, emotionless, pitch-black depths as he stared down at me. Blood clung to his black and gray stubble along his jawline and chin. "No one else can have you," he said, sounding detached as he plunged the knife back into my stomach.

I didn't know why I put my hands on his shoulders as he withdrew the knife again. I didn't know why I met his eyes or why I asked him, "Don't you love me?" I didn't know what had possessed me to say that, but it made him pause and I could have sworn I saw regret in his eyes.

I took that as my chance to ram my knee between his legs. He made a choking noise. His hand that was holding him up gave out and he fell on top of me. Shoving him to the side, I rolled off the stairs to the floor. With a hand pressed to my bleeding abdomen, I forced myself to my feet.

I made it out the open front door into the blinding

sunlight. "Help me!" I screamed that over and over again as I ran across the lawn and climbed over the wall of bushes that served as a fence between our yard and our neighbor's. Blood was leaking down the front of me and soaking into my jeans.

I will make it.

I will make it.

I told myself that over and over as I ran to my neighbor's front door. With bloody hands I rang their doorbell a dozen times. I left bloody handprints on their front door as I pounded on it until it finally opened.

The moment the elderly couple saw that it was me and that I was hurt, they let me inside. I only made it into their home a few steps before everything seemed to shut down. My legs gave out and I fell to their floor. I had fought. I had gotten out. I had nothing left. In every sense, apart from my life. I had that. As I lay there bleeding out on my terrified neighbors' floor while they called the police, I wondered if it had all been worth it.

15

THE FOUR OF THEM WERE QUIET AS THEY PROCESSED EVERY detail I'd given them from that night.

While they did, I marveled at the fact that I had not needed a drink. I hadn't been forced. That night had been what I would consider the worst level of hell and I'd bared it to them on my own. It was sometimes hard to see progress when it came to healing. What I had just done was progress impossible not to see.

Colt took my hand. "I'm proud of you, babe."

The others voiced that they were as well.

"Do you think the fight for your life was worth it?" Knox asked.

With a small smile, I got to my feet and made my way around the coffee table to him. I leaned down and pressed my lips to his in a soft, sweet kiss. "If I woke up tied to that bed tomorrow, I would fight like hell and endure everything that came after all over again, if it meant I found the four of you."

When I went to straighten, Knox grabbed me by my arm and pulled me into his lap. "I don't want us to be the reason. You have to see the value of your life on your own."

"You misunderstood me." I got more comfortable in his lap so I could look him right in the eye. "It is hard to see or find value in anything when it's dark all around you. The four of you gave me light. So I don't value my life because the four of you are in it. I value my life because the four of you showed me how. Some might find it ridiculous that it took your help to value myself again, but I think it's all right to get help sometimes." I gave him another quick kiss and tried to get up from his lap.

His arms came around me. "Where are you going?"

"I'm tired. I figured I'd head to bed," I said.

"With whom?" Creed asked.

I took them all in and I could see that they all wanted to be with me. "What if we all sleep in the living room by the fire tonight? Falling asleep to that and maybe even a movie sounds really nice."

Knox kissed my temple. "We can do that."

The next morning, I woke up somewhat peacefully. My dreams hadn't been great, but they hadn't been nightmares. I had dreamt about Logan. He had shown up at the cabin telling me that Mr. X was dead and we could come back to Arizona. It was the type of dream where you knew what was happening wasn't true, yet you still had no choice but to watch yourself make a terrible decision. I knew Mr. X wasn't dead and Dream Me was about to go back to Arizona where he'd be waiting. It was a helpless sort of dream. On the upside, I didn't wake up screaming.

Instead, I woke up between Knox and Creed. Lying on the other side of Creed was Colt and lying on Knox's other side was Keelan. Last night we had made a giant bed of blankets and pillows and slept in the living room. Despite the uncomfortable floor, I was already looking forward to when we could all sleep together again.

I was currently lying on my side facing Creed. I could hear Knox breathing evenly behind me. Maybe I was still partially asleep, or I was just simply turned on sleeping next to all my guys. Either way, I was feeling brave and bold.

I scooted closer to Creed and put my hand on his lower stomach. His shirt had ridden up in the night and a few inches of his skin were exposed just above the gray sweat-pants he loved to torture me with. I ran my fingers along that exposed skin from hipbone to hipbone. He twitched a little before his eyes opened slightly. It took him a few seconds to see me through the fog of sleep, but when he did, his eyes opened wider. He was about to open his mouth to say some-thing, and I quickly put my finger over his lips.

"Shh," I whispered as I leaned close and kissed him.

He kissed me back right away and that made me braver.

I slid my hand into his gray sweatpants beneath the blan-kets and wrapped my fingers around his cock, which was already hard. His breath hitched as I began stroking him. "Want to play out my fantasy?" I whispered against his mouth.

He gave me my answer with a tired, loopy smile. I pulled my hand from his pants and shoved off mine, along with my underwear, while still under the blankets. Then I climbed on top of him and straddled his now-bare hips. As I grabbed him and aligned him with my entrance, I noticed that he'd shoved his pants down to his knees. His hands went to my hips as I sank down on him.

"Fuck," he hissed, making me grin down at him.

I began moving my hips with slow, lazy rocks. His hands pushed up on my shirt until I helped him take it off me. I shoved his shirt up to his neck so I could run my hands up and down his chest as I picked up my pace riding him.

Creed moved his hands up to cup my breasts and play with my nipples. My head lolled back and I let out a low moan.

"Well, this was not how I expected to wake up," Keelan said.

"Really? I had a pretty good feeling something was going to happen," Knox said.

Without stopping, I looked their way. Both of them were watching, unabashed. Knox had his hands laced behind his head and Keelan was lying on his side with his head propped up on his elbow.

I glanced over at Colt next, and he was still asleep. Returning my attention to Creed, I leaned down to kiss him. "Didn't you promise to bend me over and fuck me?"

Keelan blew out a puff of air at the same time Knox let out a curse.

Creed smiled against my mouth. "Get on your hands and knees, Shi."

I climbed off of him and got into position. Creed pulled off his shirt and kicked off his pants the rest of the way. As he knelt behind me, Knox and Keelan both blurted, "Condom!"

Creed let out a curse at the same time I winced. "That was my bad. I was caught up in the moment," I said.

Keelan rolled and reached toward the end table next to the loveseat. He opened its small drawer that had surely been meant to store the remote for the TV if we'd had one and pulled out a condom. He chucked it at Creed before getting back in the position he had been lounging in. Knox and I stared at him questioningly.

Keelan shrugged. "It was you two that made living-room sex okay. I figured it'd be a good idea to have condoms within reach out here."

After Creed had the condom on, he grabbed me by my hips and pushed inside me. I let out a sigh.

Keelan chuckled. "Feel good, baby girl?"

"Yes," I whimpered.

Creed pulled out and thrust back into me. "You're fucking soaked, Shi."

"What a naughty little exhibitionist we have," Keelan said.

I groaned as I fisted the blankets. "Wouldn't that make you a voyeur?"

Keelan took in my shaking body. "I guess I am."

"I think all things Shiloh are your kink," Knox said as he took every inch of me in.

"I think it's safe to say that's all our kink," Colt said, and we all looked in his direction. He was awake and watching Creed and me just like his older brothers.

As Creed continued to rock into me, I lowered my head to the ground, moaning.

"Grab her by her hair," Keelan said. "I want to see her face when she comes."

Creed fisted my hair, and I was forced back up on my hands.

"Reach between your legs and rub your clit, Shiloh," Knox ordered.

I did and began rubbing it just how I liked to when I pleasured myself.

Creed let out a curse and his grip on me tightened.

Keelan and Knox chuckled. "I bet that tight little pussy is squeezing around you," Keelan said.

"Although she likes to act like she's appalled, Shi loves the dirty talk," Creed said.

"We know," Colt, Keelan, and Knox said at the same time.

"Stop talking and just fuck me please," I growled and that just made all four of them chuckle.

Creed brought his hand down on my butt cheek with a loud slap and started pounding into me harder.

"Creed!" I whined and I had to drop my hand from my clit to help hold myself up. "Don't stop!"

Creed chuckled again. "She went from angry to begging real quick."

Feeling vindictive now, I rocked back against him. "Keep talking and I'll make myself come instead."

Creed released my hair to hold me by both my hips. His thrusts never wavered. "Don't threaten me with a good time, Shi. I'd love to watch you spread those legs while you sink those fingers into your pussy."

His dirty mouth with the dirty visual made me clench around him.

Creed let out a hiss. "With how tight your pussy just got, I know what our next group activity is going to be."

"What a dirty girl," Keelan groaned.

Colt reached between my legs and took over rubbing my clit.

I cried out as I reached the edge where I felt like I'd barter anything just to come. With one more hard thrust and the perfect amount of pressure rubbed over my clit, I came. My arms gave out and I lowered my upper body to the ground.

As I contracted around Creed, he found his own release. "Cheese and fucking rice," he grunted as his thrusts sputtered to a stop. Creed let himself catch his breath for a few heartbeats before he pulled out of me and got up to go dispose of the condom.

I sat up on my knees and looked at my other boyfriends, feeling a tiny bit guilty.

Knox grabbed my clothes and held them out to me. "You're not ready to take on all of us and I don't think all of us are ready for it, either."

He was right. I didn't think I was ready to have sex with all four of them at once. Maybe one day when we all were, we would, but not today. I still felt bad for leaving them wanting, though.

Keelan got up and kissed the top of my head. "If we didn't want to watch, we could have left the room."

"Are you sure you didn't just stay because you knew I wanted you to?" I asked him.

"We absolutely stayed to play out that dirty fantasy of yours and we enjoyed every minute of it." Keelan walked away. "Because I enjoyed it so much, I'm going to replay you coming in my head while I go take a shower," he shot over his shoulder before going into the bathroom.

Colt snorted as he lay back and stretched. Knox shook

his head at Keelan's antics. Feeling more secure, I took my clothes from him and got dressed.

"We need to make a trip back to town. We're running low on things," Knox said at breakfast a few days later.

"I noticed that last night when I was cooking dinner," I said as I set down my fork on my plate.

Knox was standing on the other side of the kitchen island. He had already finished eating and was now focused on finishing off his coffee. "I checked the road this morning. It's clear of snow and it's not icy."

"It's been warmer the past few days," Creed said from where he sat next to me. "That's probably why."

Knox set down his coffee mug on the island. "It's a lot colder today. Because we don't know what the weather is going to be like over the next couple of days, we should probably go today."

I nodded. We hadn't been snowed in yet and we might not be. Or if we were, it might only be for a day. It was best to be prepared and it was good to stock up on things so we didn't have to travel to town as much.

"Can we all go this time?" Colt asked.

I shook my head. "I'm sorry. One of you has to stay behind. Hot identical twins are too memorable."

That made them smile. "It's such a hardship being this gorgeous sometimes," Creed said, making Colt snort.

Knox rolled his eyes.

"Cry about it when you stare at yourself in the mirror later, stud muffin," Keelan said as he carried his empty plate to the sink.

"Jealous you weren't the one Shi called hot today," Creed baited him.

Keelan turned around and leaned against the sink with a superior expression.

Before he could say something smart, I said, "Keelan's ego is big enough. Actually, all four of you know what you got going on and don't need reminding." When I was done speaking, I realized what I'd said may have come out a little harsher than I intended. "Sorry. That was rude, but true."

Creed snorted. "That was a terrible apology."

"Don't mind her. She's upset because she still hasn't heard from Logan," Knox said as he scooped up my plate and put it in the sink.

"I'm sure he'll call soon, babe," Colt said.

I didn't believe him, but I forced myself to nod anyway.

Keelan and Colt came with me to town. It was an easier trip and a little less stressful than the last one. I wasn't exhausted this time and I'd made a physical list of things we'd need to last us another couple of weeks. But the thought of being at the cabin another couple of weeks only added to the stress I was feeling about not hearing from Logan.

"Still thinking about Logan?" Keelan asked as the two of us loaded up my 4Runner with our purchases. Colt was currently in a cute coffee shop next door to the grocery store we'd just finished shopping in, getting us drinks.

"I can't help but think about Desert Stone and your lives back in Arizona. What if we have to be here for a few more weeks? Or a month?"

"Please don't stress about that, baby," Keelan pleaded,

looking directly at me. "We got everything taken care of back home. Katrina is taking care of Desert Stone and if we're not back in a month, we left her everything Micah would need to keep things running at the gym and take care of our house."

My shoulders sank a little. That did make me feel better.

Just as we finished loading everything, Colt exited the coffee shop with our drinks. Right away, I knew something wasn't right. His expression was tight and he was walking fast. "Get in the car, babe," he ordered. The sharpness and slight panic in his tone made me get in the car without question.

Colt didn't explain until we were pulled out of the parking lot and on the road back toward the cabin. "Your picture was on the news."

"What?" Keelan asked from the backseat.

"As I was waiting for our order, I watched the TV they had in there. The news was on. I was hoping to hear about the weather forecast and then they started talking about the daughter of an Arizona sheriff and her missing friends. Cassy, Gabe, and Amber's pictures popped up. And right next to them was your picture, babe. They listed your name, age, height, and what you were last seen wearing. There was also a fifty-thousand-dollar reward to whoever found the four of you."

Out of all the things he'd told us, I could only focus on one. "Cassy is missing?"

Colt let out a curse as he rubbed the back of his neck. "Before you showed up at Desert Stone to save me, I was in and out of consciousness, but I think I heard the sheriff talking to X or leaving him a message. I think he said X had Cassy and if he didn't give her back, he would kill you. I think he used me as a trap so he could give you to X in exchange for Cassy."

"If Mr. X is the reason Cassy is missing, she's dead. Gabe and Amber are undoubtedly dead, too," I said.

"Why kill them?" Keelan asked.

"Because he loves me, and they were a threat to me, and he's crazy."

That seemed to be a good enough answer, because the conversation moved on.

"So what are we going to do with you being on the news?" Colt asked.

I sighed, at a total loss. "I can't come back to town."

Colt reached over to put a comforting hand on my thigh.

Keelan leaned forward between my seat and Colt's to grab his coffee from the drink carrier Colt was holding in his lap. "Do you think anyone recognized you while we were inside the store?"

"I kept my head down," I said. That didn't guarantee anything, though. "I'll try calling Logan again when we get back."

After we got home and put away almost everything we had bought, I took what needed to go in my room. I had bought everything to bleach my hair again, among a few other toiletries. I set the bags with my purchases inside on my dresser. I intended to put them away after I made my call to Logan.

Sitting on my bed, I dialed Logan's number on the burner phone. His phone rang and rang until it went to voicemail. I let out a frustrated growl as I hung up. Logan had told me not to call Ian unless I had no choice, but I couldn't take it anymore. I clicked on Ian's contact saved in the phone and put the phone to my ear. It rang and rang until it, too, went to voicemail.

"Ian, it's me. Call me." I left a message before hanging up and tossing my phone on the bed.

16

I WOKE UP EARLY THE NEXT DAY AFTER DREAMING ABOUT going to Logan's funeral. Mr. X had killed him while I was safe and hidden away at the cabin. Ian was the one who'd invited me to it and even though Mr. X was still searching for me, I risked going. As Logan's casket was being lowered into the ground, I spotted Mr. X standing with the crowd of mourners, whose faces I could not see. He was watching me with an evil, proud smirk. *Dream Me is dumb,* I thought as I climbed out of bed and put on some clothes to run in.

After I was dressed, I made my way through the quiet cabin and went down to the basement to run on the treadmill that was among the few pieces of exercise equipment down there. The basement wasn't much. It had bare concrete walls and concrete flooring. The small personal gym had a treadmill, an exercise bike, and an elliptical. On one wall there were a few shelves of board games and up against another there was a folded-up ping-pong table, but I had no clue where the paddles and balls to it were.

Running felt good. It helped ease some of the stress that

was building due to not hearing from both Logan and Ian. I hated not knowing what was going on. I hated not knowing if everyone we knew was all right or not. I constantly felt like I was fighting with myself on what to do. Keep us safe and stay out of what might be happening back in Arizona, or wherever Mr. X was wreaking havoc, or give in and join the fight. A few weeks ago, I would have never considered putting myself at risk to help hunt down Mr. X, but I was getting tired of this type of life. Was it greedy to want more? I was happy. We were safe. That should have been enough, but what kind of life were we living if it was always over-shadowed with fear?

Living in fear isn't living. Knox had taught me that.

Maybe I was just feeling cooped-up and needed to get out.

Hoping that was it, after breakfast I grabbed a box of bullets from the safe and one of my rifles from where I kept it loaded and ready to use by the front door. Now that I knew the guys knew how to shoot, I'd put guns in almost every room of the cabin. There was a pistol in each of the bedrooms, a rifle over the fireplace, and the one I was hold-ing. Knox had his pistol, too, but I didn't know where he kept it.

"I'm going to go shooting," I announced to Colt and Creed. Knox and Keelan were working out in the basement again. "Anyone want to come with me?"

"I'll come," Colt said.

"You two go. I'm going to go get a workout in with Knox and Keelan," Creed said.

While Colt went to put on warmer clothes, I found some empty cans to use for target practice. I put the cans and box of bullets in a plastic grocery bag to make them easier to carry. When I was done, Colt was ready and the two of us headed out. We went back to that clearing with the knocked-over tree. It had snowed out and everything was covered with fresh powder. Snow crunched under our boots as we walked until the cabin was long out of sight.

Like we had done before, Colt and I took turns shooting. Colt had really good aim and we quickly started competing to see who could hit the most cans.

"Want to add stakes?" I asked as I stared down the scope on top of the rifle.

He chuckled. "The last time I made bets with you, you cheated."

I grinned an evil little grin. "If you win, I'll get down on my knees and make it up to you."

"And if you win?"

"You'll get down on your knees for me," I said and pulled the trigger. Through the scope, I saw my can go flying. Lowering the rifle so it pointed to the ground, I turned to face Colt.

He was smiling while staring at the cans. "So I'll win either way."

My evil grin turned into a naughty one. "So will I."

Our little competition had almost been a tie, but in the end, Colt had beaten me and I wasn't mad about it. I knelt in the snow in front of him and licked, sucked, and made myself gag on him until he was spilling down my throat.

Before I could think to stand up, he pushed me down on the cold snow and warmed me up by burying his head between my legs. By the time I came, the back of my clothes were wet from the snow. I didn't care. It was worth it.

As we were cleaning up the cans and spent rifle shells by putting them all in the bag I'd brought, we heard the distinct growl of a bear nearby. I picked up my rifle and spun around as I searched for the source. I spotted a black bear walking toward us about thirty yards away.

I didn't want to shoot it, but I didn't want it to come any closer. Pointing the barrel of my rifle toward the sky, I fired off a round. The loud noise spooked the bear and it took off in another direction.

Colt came to stand next to me with the cans in his hands. "That could have been bad."

I scoffed in disbelief. "Yeah."

"I thought bears hibernated in the winter?"

"Me, too. Let's get moving," I said as I grabbed the bag I had dropped.

We finished collecting everything we had brought and began heading back, holding hands. I carried the rifle in my free hand. In his, Colt carried the grocery bag of cans, the box that still had a few bullets inside, and all the shells the rifle had ejected each time we'd fired a round.

"I'm counting that as the date you owed me," he said to me.

It took me a moment to understand what he was talking about. Then I remembered it was from a bet we'd placed while running the track at school. "I'll count the snow as the ice cream you promised to take me to get."

"Or we can eat some ice cream when we get back to the cabin."

"That's right! I forgot we picked some up yester—"

My words were cut off by the distant echo of gunshots.

Colt and I froze. Then another shot went off and it sounded like they were coming from the cabin. We both took off running. I clutched my rifle in both of my hands. There were four rounds loaded in it and I didn't want to risk dropping it.

We ran as fast as we could, but we were a good distance away from the cabin. As we were about to come out of a cluster of trees into a large, snowy clearing, we both spotted Knox running and about sixty feet behind him was Sheriff McAllister.

The sheriff stopped running and aimed his gun at the sky before pulling the trigger. Colt and I stopped in our tracks. I quickly brought my rifle up and aimed it at the sheriff. Staring at them through the scope, I saw Knox stop running and slowly turn to face the sheriff.

Sheriff McAllister had his pistol aimed at Knox, which made my heart try to lodge itself in my throat.

"Where is she?" I barely heard the sheriff yell.

Knox didn't answer and that seemed to piss the sheriff off. I read what the sheriff intended to do, and I saw him curl his finger over the trigger of his gun. I could not hesitate this time.

Don't miss, I told myself as I aimed for the sheriff's neck and pulled the trigger.

The sheriff's hand went to his throat before he fell back into the snow. Knox turned in our direction as I lowered the barrel of the rifle. When I started to walk toward them, so did Colt. As we made our way over, I pulled back the bolt on the rifle to allow another bullet to enter the chamber before sliding the bolt forward and locking it back into place.

I eyed Knox from head to toe, making sure he wasn't hurt. He looked fine. "Was there anyone else with him?" I asked in a voice that sounded cold and detached even to my own ears.

"He came with two others," Knox said as he stared at me. "They're dead."

"Are Keelan and Creed okay?" Colt asked.

Knox nodded.

That satisfied me enough to walk away and head over to the sheriff. He was still alive, bleeding out into the snow, struggling to breathe. His eyes locked on me as I approached.

"Please," he gasped out as he put a trembling hand into his pants pocket. He pulled out a cell phone and held it out to me. "Save—" He coughed. Blood and saliva shot out of his mouth and rolled down his cheek. "Save Cassy."

I debated whether or not I wanted to tell him that she was more than likely dead. But if I did, this moment would haunt me even more than it already would. I took the phone from him. "I'll try," I forced myself to say. It was all the kindness I could offer him in his last moments. It was probably more than he would have offered me.

I held my tears back until I saw the life leave his eyes— the life I'd taken.

Cheese and fucking rice!

I walked away on unsteady legs, and I gasped in cold air.

"Shiloh?" Knox said at the same time Colt said, "Babe?"

I just kept walking aimlessly, tears rolling down my cheeks. My knees buckled, I stumbled, and I was going down.

Arms caught me from behind before I hit the ground. "You did what you had to." Knox's deep voice filled my ear and tried to soothe me. He held me tight as I cried. "It's all right. You had to."

I knew that and I wouldn't take it back even if I could, but that didn't mean it felt any less terrible. A soul-broken sob barreled out of me. Colt took my rifle from my hand and set it on the ground before putting himself in front of me and wrapping his arms around me and Knox. They held me until I stopped crying.

～

While the three of us walked back to the cabin, Knox told us what had happened. He, Creed, and Keelan had just finished up their workout in the basement and as they'd headed toward the front of the cabin, Creed had thrown snowballs at Knox and Keelan, which had started a battle. To avoid getting hit, Creed had run inside the cabin. Knox said it had been a cowardly move, but it had saved them.

Just as Creed had gone inside, an Arizona police car had driven up to the cabin. Sheriff McAllister and two others had gotten out of the car. None of them had worn a uniform; they'd been in civilian clothes, and they'd been armed. One of the sheriff's friends had asked Knox and Keelan where I was, or more specifically, "Where's the girl?"

Keelan and Knox had said I wasn't there. The two friends had looked to the sheriff, who had then nodded at them, and they'd pulled their pistols from their side holsters. They'd pointed their guns at Knox and Keelan and demanded again to know where I was.

Then a shot had sounded in the distance. It was the shot I'd fired to spook the bear.

"I guess we have our answer," the sheriff had said. "I'll let you take care of things here." The sheriff had then started walking in my and Colt's direction while the other two had held Keelan and Knox at gunpoint.

Knox said he'd known that they were going to shoot them. He had seen it in their eyes when they'd glanced at each other.

Before they'd been able to shoot, a shot had rung out behind Knox and Keelan. One of the men had fallen dead. Knox and Keelan had run in opposite directions to get away. The guy who'd still been alive had shot at Keelan while backing away toward the police car. Keelan had gotten nicked in the thigh before he'd been able to hide behind his Jeep. While the guy had been focused shooting at Keelan, Creed had ripped open the front door of the cabin and shot him with the rifle I had taught him how to shoot.

After making sure Keelan was all right and hearing where Colt and I were from Creed, Knox had taken off to try to get to us before the sheriff. Because the sheriff hadn't known exactly where I'd been, Knox had been able to get ahead of the sheriff, but not by enough.

When we made it back to the cabin, Creed was sitting on the front porch looking as torn-up as I felt. Keelan was sitting with him, a kitchen towel tied around his thigh.

I eyed the two dead bodies and recognized them as the two police officers who had pulled me and Logan over when we'd been on our way to my school. They had done it to intimidate me for the sheriff, but as soon as they had seen Logan's badge, they had balked.

I rushed the rest of the way to my guys. "Are you all right?" I asked Keelan.

He nodded and glanced at Creed, who was frowning at the ground. "What happened to the sheriff?"

"Shiloh killed him," Knox said with a low voice.

I knelt in front of Creed and cupped his cheeks. "I'm so sorry you had to do that."

His eyes drifted to me slowly. "I had to." His voice came out empty yet angry.

"It still feels terrible," I said.

He nodded and pulled me closer.

I straddled his lap and hugged his neck as his arms wrapped around my ribs tightly. "I'm sorry," I whispered over and over to him.

17

I CALLED LOGAN AT LEAST TEN TIMES WITHIN AN HOUR. When he still didn't pick up, I called Ian as I paced my room. By the fifth time I called him, Ian finally picked up.

"Hello," said a weak voice and I could faintly hear a beeping sound in the background.

"Ian?" I said.

"Shiloh." He let out a grunt and I could hear him moving. "Why are you calling me? It's not safe."

"Well, I'm not safe where I am. Where is Logan?"

He let out a sigh. "How are you not safe? Logan said you went to a safe house."

"Sheriff McAllister found me." I paused to steel myself to say what I had to next. "I had to kill him and the men he brought with him." I didn't bring up that Creed had killed the sheriff's buddies. It wasn't important right now. "My location has been compromised. I have three dead bodies rotting outside and I don't know what to do."

Ian let out a curse. A lot of them. "If McAllister found

you, then X knows where you are. You need to get out of there now."

"The sheriff and Mr. X are still working together even though Mr. X took his daughter?"

Ian was quiet for a heartbeat. "Tell me everything you know, kid."

I told him everything that had happened from when I'd started to sense things weren't right to after I'd saved Colt and driven to Colorado. "Now it's your turn to tell me why Logan hasn't called me."

He went quiet again. "Logan busted his phone before we boarded our planes out of Arizona. To make it harder to figure out that we were coming from Arizona, we flew separately and picked flights with a lot of layovers. Logan didn't get your messages until after he landed at where Mr. X was last spotted, which was in Tennessee, and he replaced his phone. By the time he listened to your messages, it was the day after the attack on your friend. Right around the time he found out, I found out because word of what had happened had reached me. We booked direct flights right back to Arizona. Before we boarded the plane back, Logan checked your tracker and saw that you were almost to your safe house. When we landed back in Arizona, he checked again and saw that you had made it. We threw ourselves into the investigation after that. We reviewed the video feed from your house. Your cameras caught X going in and out of your house many times and as you suspected, you were in the house with him without knowing it. He got in through the spare bedroom window that you found open. I'm pretty sure McAllister was the one who left it open for him when he broke into your house the last time."

"Do you know how the sheriff got in touch with Mr. X?" I asked him.

"We didn't know McAllister and X were connected until a few days ago," he said as if frustrated. "Before we found out McAllister was involved, we discovered that someone had created multiple social media profiles with your Arizona driver's license photo. The bios of these profiles said that you lived in Arizona and gave a phone number. We're pretty sure that's how the two connected."

I thought back to the last time the sheriff had broken into my house. "The sheriff had mentioned to me once that he found it intriguing that I didn't take part in any social media. He also said he couldn't find a single picture of me other than my driver's license. I think he was toying with me because he was already in contact with Mr. X by then."

"Sounds like it." Ian let out another sigh. "Listen, kid, I need to tell you something and I need you not to do anything dangerous because of it."

That instantly put me on edge. "What?"

"We didn't know McAllister was working with X or that X had taken his daughter until a few days ago. Up until that point, even though he was on thin ice because of what he had done to you, he was helpful and very involved in the investigation. He played the *my nephew and my daughter's friend are missing* card. Everyone believed him. Even Logan and me. Logan was certain that the kids' disappearance was connected to X. They went missing right after they attacked you, and we lifted a print off of Jacob's suicide letter. It belonged to X."

"I already knew he killed Jacob. The note was Mr. X's words."

"It was definitely his brand of crazy," Ian grumbled.

"The only thing that stood out about McAllister was that he kept giving us excuses to keep us from interviewing his daughter. He said he had sent her to a family member out of state to keep her safe. Logan sort of sympathized with him on that, but I found it odd. When he finally agreed to let us meet her, he said it had to be at his house. Logan and I agreed to go there."

Oh, no! "It was a trap."

"Fuck, kid, I don't know how to tell you this."

Before my legs could give out, I sat on the edge of the bed. "Logan's dead, isn't he?"

"I don't know," he said. "We walked into that house and McAllister fucking maced us. I couldn't see and the next thing I know, I'm being stabbed. I fell to the ground and all I could do was listen. Logan struggled and fought, even though he was as blind as I was. He was yelling. Shit was breaking. It took a while, but McAllister was able to hurt Logan enough to make him go down. As soon as he did, he called X and asked where to bring Logan. I had lost so much blood and I couldn't fucking see, all I could do was lay there. I think McAllister seemed to forget about me because as soon as X told him where to meet him, he was focused on leaving with Logan. I came in and out of consciousness quite a bit as he took him away. When I was really able to come to, I was alone in his house. I searched for my phone, I didn't have it anymore. I had to drag myself out of his house and to his neighbors. I don't know how long it took me or how long it took for EMS to get me to the hospital. I had to have surgery and didn't wake up until late last night. During the time I was out, McAllister took over the hunt for X. He added you as one of the missing kids and used the disappearance of his daughter—a sheriff's daughter

—to get more media coverage to spread your picture far and wide.

"By the time I woke up and reported what had happened to me and Logan, McAllister was gone. I thought he skipped town. I didn't think he got a lead on where to find you. Someone must've seen you and called it in."

I just sat there quietly processing. "Mr. X has Logan?"

"I believe so."

"There is a good chance that he's dead," I said in a vacant voice.

"Or X is going to use Logan to lure you to him."

I could break down right now. I really could. Or I could stay strong and get my family somewhere safe. "We can't stay here."

"No. I'm going to send agents to come and get you. Can you find somewhere safe until then?"

"There's a hotel in town," I said.

"Which town and hotel?" he asked.

I told him.

"If it will make you feel any better, your friend is going to be okay," he said.

"Which friend?"

"Isabelle. She's still in the hospital but she's no longer in critical condition. Doctors say with a little bit of physical therapy, she'll make a full recovery."

I stared up at the ceiling as tears flooded my eyes. It took a tremendous effort to keep myself composed. "Thank you for telling me that."

"Be safe, kid." He hung up after that.

I knew I couldn't just sit there. It was just really hard to move. Isabelle was alive. I was so unbelievably happy about that, but the news of Logan was tearing me apart.

I inhaled deeply and exhaled slowly. "Okay." I repeated the process of breathing like that again before I nodded and forced myself to stand.

As soon as I started to head out of my room to go tell the guys, that phone Sheriff McAllister had given to me started vibrating in the pocket of my sweatshirt. I pulled it out and the screen read *X*.

I swallowed as I hit the green button to answer it and then brought it to my ear. "Hello?"

Mr. X's haunting voice filled my ear through the phone. "Hello, my Shiloh."

I was in no rush after my call with Mr. X, and at the same time, I was. Walking into the living room where the guys were waiting for me, I kept my hands in my sweatshirt pockets because I couldn't stop fisting them. I took a seat next to Creed on the couch. "I got ahold of Ian." After announcing that, I explained everything that Ian had told me. As I spoke, I noticed Keelan had changed his pants. I had given Knox supplies to help bandage him up while I'd made my calls.

"So we need to leave?" Knox asked.

I nodded.

"What about the bodies outside?" Creed asked.

"Ian will take care of it." I hoped.

The four of them started to get up to go collect what they would need to leave. I grabbed Creed's wrist before he could walk away. He eyed my hand on his wrist and sat back down.

I waited for the other three to leave the room before I

turned my body to face him. I took his hands in mine. "I love you so much."

He frowned. "I'm going to be okay."

He thought I was telling him I loved him because of what had happened earlier with the sheriff's men. That was all right.

"I wanted to be a chef, to be a wife and a mother. I wanted those things, but when Mr. X took my family away, I made myself stop wanting those things because I thought if I didn't want them, I couldn't be disappointed for not getting them." I stared down at our hands, and I squeezed his. "On Halloween, when I was dancing and having so much fun with Isabelle, I let myself envision a future. I let myself want more."

He was still frowning. "And what do you want?"

"I want what I wanted before, and I want it with the four of you. I want to spend the rest of my life placing bets with you and Colt, I want to spar with Keelan, and I want to rebel against Knox. He may act like he doesn't like it, but we all know that he enjoys it."

A small smile tugged at the corner of Creed's mouth. "He loves that you won't back down and that you're not afraid to push back."

I returned his small smile with my own. It was a little forced, but I managed to give him one. "I want family meals, to celebrate birthdays, and to wake up every morning next to one of you. I want to laugh with you and fight with you and love you until I'm old. And one day, *many* years from now, I want babies who have beautiful blond hair and either aquamarine or golden-brown eyes. I want all of that. Desperately."

His eyes searched mine. "Not that I'm not happy to hear

all of that. I am. I want those things with you, too, but why are you telling me this?"

I let go of his hands to cup his face. "I'm telling you so you know—so that it may help you when you feel upset. That I love you so much and would do anything to have that future with you."

He closed his eyes with a sigh and grabbed my wrists. "I'm going to be fine, Shi. I was in shock, but I know I had to do what I had to, or they would have killed my brothers."

This is okay, I told myself. Hopefully, he would understand later.

I leaned forward and kissed him.

Please forgive me.

I pulled away and stood. "We should get ready to leave."

Creed stood as well, and we both headed for the hall. As soon as we entered it, we saw Knox standing there, leaning against the wall. Creed passed him to go into the spare bedroom to collect his things. I avoided Knox's stare as I also passed him and entered my room. I grabbed my go bag off of the trunk at the foot of my bed. I had taken it out of the safe before calling Logan and Ian. Since the sheriff had found us, I'd known I would need it again. As I unzipped it, I heard Knox close the bedroom door.

"That was quite a talk," he said.

I grabbed a few days' worth of clothes from the dresser and stuffed them in the bag. "He had to kill those men because of me." It wasn't a lie. I did feel terrible he'd had to do that, but I didn't have the room in me to feel the guilt of it yet.

"Is that really why you said those things to him? As a way to make him feel better?"

No. I'd said all that because I knew he would take what I

had to do the hardest. I had hoped to help him understand that so long as the threat of Mr. X existed, we would never be free to have that beautiful future. I hoped that by telling him my most vulnerable desires, he would understand that I wouldn't do anything to jeopardize them if I didn't have to.

"Yes," I lied, and if Knox could tell, he didn't call me out on it.

18

We drove both my 4Runner and Keelan's Jeep into town. Knox checked us in to a hotel room. I told him we weren't staying more than a night before Ian's…colleagues came. I wore a hat and a pair of sunglasses that Colt had been nice enough to get me from a gas station on the way here. I didn't want to cause a disturbance if someone recognized me from TV.

The four of us made our way to our room. I left my go bag and guns in my 4Runner and only brought in what I would need for the night.

As we rode the elevator up, in a very nice hotel, I said, "I wish we could go out to dinner."

"That would be nice," Colt said.

"It's probably best you stay in the room," Knox said.

"A few of us can go pick something up and bring it back," Keelan suggested.

"Or we can order room service and enjoy cable TV," Creed said. "Maybe they have the cooking channel, and we can watch that chef you fangirl over."

I actually smiled. "If you understood who Bobby Flay was, you would fangirl, too. Even my mom would swoon when we'd watch him."

"So not only do you admire him, but you find him attractive as well?" Creed asked.

"He's old enough to be your father, babe," Colt said.

I shrugged. "I have a thing for blonds."

Keelan snorted and before the twins could say anything more, the elevator doors opened. We made our way down to the suite Knox had gotten us. After going inside and looking around, we saw that it was a two-bedroom suite with one room with a king-sized bed and another room with two queen beds. Between the two rooms was a small kitchen and living-room area with a couch that pulled out into another bed.

After we set down our things, we all met in the living room. I sat in the center of the couch. Creed sat on one side of me with the remote in his hand. Keelan sat on my other side. Colt took a seat in one of the two armchairs. The three of them all let out a sigh. They were tired both emotionally and physically. Running and hiding did that to you.

Knox joined us in the living room last. "I didn't find a room service menu. Why don't Colt and I go pick something up?"

"How will you know what we want?" Creed asked.

Knox looked to me. "Can I take the burner phone and I'll call the room when I find a place?"

I nodded. "I put it on the kitchen counter."

Knox grabbed the pad of paper and pen that had the hotel's logo on it and wrote down the room number and the hotel's phone number. Then he and Colt left.

Creed flipped through the channels on the TV. When he

came upon one of our favorite cooking competition shows, he said, "Here we go," and set the remote down. Just seeing how the cooking show seemed to relax him, I found myself smiling. He caught me with my goofy smile and pulled me to his chest before leaning back. Keelan grabbed my feet and set them on his good thigh.

"How's your leg?" I asked him.

"It's fine. It's not nearly as bad as your arm was," he said.

I was pretty sure he was lying. By the amount of blood I'd seen on the towel he'd used to wrap around it, I was pretty sure it was.

It was close to an hour until the room's phone rang. I got up to answer it. "Did you two get lost?"

"We had trouble deciding on a place," Knox said. He then told me about the place they were at and what was on the menu. I passed on everything he told me to Creed and Keelan. We told Knox what we wanted and before we hung up, he asked me if I would like any dessert.

"Ice cream, please," I said and our call ended.

It was nearly another hour before Knox and Colt returned with all the food. The rest of the evening was as wonderful as we could make it. We didn't leave the living room. We ate dinner and then ice cream while watching food competitions. During that time, I refused to think of anything else other than the four of them and being in the moment with them.

As the night grew late, Creed fell asleep on the couch, and I pretended to do the same with my head on his chest. I listened as the other three whispered about going to bed and being careful not to wake us. One of them put a blanket on top of Creed and me before heading off toward the bedrooms.

I listened to Creed's heartbeat for most of the night and when the sun was about an hour from rising, I quietly climbed off of him. I had set everything I would need to leave on the kitchen counter along with the pen and pad of paper that Knox had used. I wrote out a detailed note explaining everything.

They knew Logan had been taken by Mr. X, but they didn't know that Mr. X had called me on the sheriff's phone threatening to kill Logan if I didn't come to him. To prove that Logan was alive, he'd let Logan talk to me.

"Shiloh. Don't come. Don't give this fucker—"

He had been cut off when Mr. X had returned to the line and told me where to find him.

If I knew Mr. X like I thought I did, he would kill Logan as soon as I got there. I was walking into a trap that might be pointless. However, I couldn't live with myself if I didn't try.

I finished my note by thanking them for finding me, saving me, and loving me. I explained how much I loved them and to please forgive me. That I wasn't just doing this to try to save Logan, but to free us from a life filled with danger, running, and fear.

I put the note on the coffee table for Creed to see when he woke up. Then I grabbed my keys to my 4Runner and my burner phone from the kitchen counter and snuck out.

I drove for twenty-six hours. I stopped once at a cheap hotel for six hours to sleep so I wouldn't be exhausted when I returned to my childhood home in Maryland. Driving through the town I'd grown up in felt nostalgic yet strange.

Who I used to be when I'd lived here was not who I was now.

As I pulled into my old neighborhood, my hands began to shake. I drove by my house once without stopping and parked down another street. Grabbing my burner phone, I dialed Ian's number. He had called me multiple times since I'd left Colorado.

The line rang and rang until it went to voicemail. I said, "For someone who has been blowing up my phone, you chose a crappy time to not answer. I'm doing something reckless, despite you telling me not to. I'm in Maryland. Mr. X found a way to get ahold of me and told me I had to come or he'd kill Logan. When you get this, feel free to send the police to my house here."

I hung up and got out of my car. I unzipped my sweatshirt and tossed it in the car before making my way to the trunk. The chill in the air made my exposed arms break out in goosebumps. Before arriving in my hometown, I'd made sure to stop by a few stores. My pink hair was in a tight bun to make sure it was harder to grab. I was wearing black cargo pants with boots to be able to move around quicker and easier. I had on a loose black T-shirt to hide the belly band holster that held a pistol behind my back. After opening the trunk, I grabbed a seven-inch survival knife with a fixed blade and tucked it into one of my boots. I grabbed my shoulder holster that held another pistol and put it on. Lastly, I put a spare magazine in one of the pockets in my pants.

As I went to close the trunk, something shiny peeking out from under the mat in the trunk caught my eye. I lifted the corner of the mat and found a quarter-sized disk with a well-known apple-shaped logo on it. There was an AirTag in my trunk. Questions rattled my brain. Who'd put it in my car? How long had it been there? Had Logan done it? It obviously hadn't been put in my car by the sheriff or Mr. X or they would have showed up at the cabin a lot sooner. It must have been Logan. Was my car a backup in case anything happened to my ankle tracker, which I currently had hidden in my boot?

I supposed it didn't matter right now. I tossed the AirTag back in the trunk and shut it. Because I was parked a street over from my childhood home, I cut through the property that was directly behind mine. If the owners happened to see me and called the police, then so be it.

There were a lot of trees and bushes that framed the large lot my house sat on. I tried to stick close to them in hope of staying unseen as I made my way to the house. I didn't want Mr. X to see me coming; he was already more than prepared for me.

Before I'd left the hospital after Mr. X had killed my family, Logan had hired people to clean, fix up, and lock down the house. Nails had been removed from the doors and windows downstairs. The missing doorknobs had been replaced. The blood had been cleaned away. Because we hadn't had time to go through my and my family's belongings, everything had been kept where it had been, and all the furniture had been covered with white cloth to help preserve it until I could go through it.

The elderly couple who lived next door and had helped save me had agreed to keep an eye on the house and been given keys to do so. If anything were to happen, Logan had given them an email to reach him by. In the past year and a half, we hadn't heard from them. So I assumed everything was good with the house. I really hoped they hadn't noticed Mr. X hanging around.

I first tried to get in through the back door using my house keys kept in my go bag. The door unlocked but wouldn't open. It was nailed shut.

Bastard!

I knew the game he was playing. He wanted to control the way I came in and possibly my escape. And he was probably trying to recreate the night he'd killed my family.

I didn't bother trying to go through any of the windows or the garage. I walked around the house to the front door. Before opening the door, I took my pistol from my shoulder holster, aimed it out in front of me, and reached for the door handle. Steeling myself with a deep breath and slow exhale, I opened the door. Slowly, I pushed it inward and stepped into the place that had haunted my dreams since the night I'd barely escaped alive.

19

Stepping inside, I could hear my younger self say, "I'm home."

The first thing I noticed when I came in was the smell. It smelled like rotting meat, and I had the overwhelming urge to gag. Apart from the stench, nothing was unusual. It was quiet. The lights were off, but it was the middle of the day and light was coming in through the windows.

I left the door open behind me as I moved farther inside. Why not? If Mr. X wanted it closed, I was sure he'd close it. Because I couldn't resist, I took a few steps to the left to look in the living room. As expected, the furniture was covered with white cloth.

Unexpectedly, I found the reason for the terrible smell. It took a lot of effort not to scream. I quickly looked away from the horrific sight and took a second to restrengthen my ability to bury what I was feeling.

I made myself look back into the living room and took in the scene Mr. X had recreated for me. Laid out in the same spots my parents had been killed in were Gabe and Amber.

Gabe was laid in the same position on the couch and butchered in the same exact manner as my dad had been. Amber was on the floor. There wasn't blood surrounding her, but it was obvious that she had been stabbed to death as my mom had been. They were both wearing the costumes they had been wearing on Halloween. Their faces were permanently etched with fear.

Even though they had done awful things to me, they didn't deserve what Mr. X had done to them.

I glanced up the stairs. If Gabe and Amber were where my parents had been killed, who had Mr. X placed where Shayla had been killed? Gun still held out in front of me, I began making my way up.

Before I reached the top, the hall came into view and there stood Mr. X with Logan kneeling in front of him. Mr. X was holding a knife to Logan's throat. As I came to stand on the landing at the edge of the hall, Shayla's death replayed in my mind.

Logan looked half dead already. He was severely beaten and bloody. His face was cut, purple, and swollen. There were large cuts on his arms, and he looked like he had been stabbed in his stomach. He appeared so weak that the only thing holding him upright was the grip Mr. X had on his hair.

Mr. X was in all black like me, wearing another Desert Stone hoodie. What I noticed now that I hadn't at the gym was that he had put on some muscle. It appeared I hadn't been the only one working on making myself stronger. There was also a small scar on his cheek where I had stabbed him with the pen.

An ominous smile stretched across his mouth, causing that scar to wrinkle. "Welcome home, Shiloh."

"Shi," Logan groaned.

Mr. X fisted his hair and pulled his head back, exposing Logan's throat. "Did you like what I left you downstairs?" Mr. X asked me.

I didn't answer. All I did was hold my gun aimed at his head and stare my monster, my demon, my boogeyman right in the eye. I was not who I had been. I was stronger. I was smarter. I would not give him my fear any longer. If he were to try and take from me again, he would only have my rage.

I didn't know what I showed on my face, but his evil smile shrank a little. "At first, I thought I'd put that horrible girl here where I killed your sister. Then, when your uncle fell into my lap, I decided that it would be more fitting to cut the truly last tether holding you back from me."

I lowered my gun with a sigh. "How boring." It may have been my voice, but it was Shayla's tone and words I was conjuring.

Mr. X's smile dropped completely.

"I don't think you truly love me," I said.

The surprise that showed on his face told me what I was doing was working. What I had learned when Mr. X had stabbed me and again when he'd almost raped me in the middle of the night was that when I played into his fantasy, I gained the power.

"Why couldn't you have done something new?" I asked with a somber look. I took a few steps forward and pointed the barrel of my gun to my temple. "If you really wanted to recreate the death of my sister, then maybe I should be the one to die here. After all, I look just like her."

Mr. X's knife fell away from Logan's neck and he let go of his hair. Logan fell forward on his hands with a grunt.

Mr. X took a step toward me. "I do love you."

I smiled. "I know you do." I moved the barrel of my gun

away from my head and aimed it at Mr. X's. There was no doubt or hesitation when I pulled the trigger.

Mr. X ducked, but my bullet grazed his cheek and ear. I didn't know if he felt the pain because right away, he threw his knife at me. I too had to duck, and in that time, he charged for me while pulling another chef's knife out from the pouch pocket of his hoodie. He came at me too quickly to bring my gun up to aim at his head. In a split second, I came to the decision to drop my gun and brace. He lifted his hand, clutching the knife as if to strike as he came at me. I caught his wrist as he was bringing it down with one hand, fisted his hoodie with my other, and pulled him down to the ground. As I brought us down, I brought one foot up and shoved it into his stomach. When my back slammed down onto the carpet, I thrust my leg—the strongest part of my body—up into Mr. X and propelled his body over my head, which was where I knew the stairs would be. Mr. X flipped and tumbled down the stairs. I prayed to whatever deity would listen that his neck would break.

Halfway down the stairs he dropped his knife and caught hold of the banister. At the speed he was going down, combined with his weight, the newel he'd grabbed snapped and he continued tumbling down to the foyer.

I scooped up my gun and got to my feet. Running to Logan, I shoved my gun in my shoulder holster. I quickly grabbed his arm and put it around the back of my neck. "I need you to help me," I said to him as I pulled him up to stand.

He helped me a little to get him to his feet. "You need to get out of here."

"Not without you. Now walk," I ordered as I led us farther down the hall, away from the stairs.

He walked, and better than I'd thought he would, which would make what I was going to make him do next easier. In the ceiling in front of my parents' bedroom door was the pull-down ladder that led to the attic.

"Can you reach that?" I asked Logan as I pointed to the small metal ring that dangled a few inches from the ceiling.

Logan reached up and hooked his fingers in the ring. When he yanked down, the ring pulled a rope out of the ceiling until it went taut, and the attic door opened.

I took over for Logan and opened the attic door enough to pull down the ladder. "Climb, Logan, and hurry."

While Logan struggled but did his best to climb up the ladder, I took my knife out of my boot and cut the ring and rope from the door, all while staring toward the stairs.

As soon as Logan was far enough up, he pulled himself into the attic by rolling his body inside. "Hurry, Shi," he said between pants.

I returned my knife to my boot and started to push up the folding ladder. "I'm not coming up."

"What?" he said and tried to roll over to look down at me.

"Stay there until I come for you. If you try to come out, I will shoot you in your legs and lock you in a closet."

"Damn it, Shi!"

I ignored his arguments as I finished closing the attic door. Without the rope to pull it down, he should be safe up there. Turning to face the other end of the hall, where the stairs were, I pulled out my gun from my shoulder holster and headed in that direction.

When I reached the stairs, I glanced down at the foyer. Mr. X was nowhere to be seen and it looked like he'd shut the front door. Which meant he was hiding somewhere downstairs. I racked my brain on what to do as I went down a few steps. This house was so big and boxy. The moment I started to look for him, he could come upstairs and try to look for Logan.

The sun coming in from the windows above the front door made the crystal chandelier that hung above the foyer sparkle. Then I eyed the lights on the top of the hall wall leading to the kitchen. I aimed my gun at the chain that anchored the chandelier to the ceiling and pulled the trigger twice. The chain snapped and the beautiful light fixture fell. Glass shattered and scattered, covering the foyer floor.

I moved down the stairs. "Ooooh, Mr. X!" I shouted through the house. I was no longer the mouse in this terrifying game he forced me to play; I was the cat. I paused my descent to aim at the light fixture on the hall wall and shot it. More glass hit the ground. "Come out! Come out, wherever you are!" I shot the next light farther down the hall.

As I stepped off the stairs, my boots crunched on the glass. Gun out in front of me, I looked into the living room. He wasn't in there. Beyond the living room was my dad's office. It was dark because it didn't have any windows. Going in there looking for him would be too much of a risk. It would be better to draw him out into the open. So I moved across the foyer to my mom's office. Glass crunched under my boots with each step. I glanced into the Jack-and-Jill bathroom before moving to the other side of the office. My mom's desk faced the foyer. I knelt behind it. From my vantage point, I could see into the foyer, a little bit of the living room, and the entrance to the bathroom.

Now we'd see who would catch who.

20

I DIDN'T KNOW HOW MUCH TIME HAD PASSED. TEN MINUTES? Fifteen? Maybe it had been an hour and I couldn't tell. Time moved and felt differently when adrenaline bumped through your whole body and your heart pounded out of fear in your chest.

The sound of glass crunching echoed in the hall near the kitchen. I stood up from behind the desk, gun aimed toward the foyer as I listened. I didn't hear the sound of glass crunching again. Therefore, the only route Mr. X could take would be through the Jack-and-Jill bathroom. I pointed my gun toward there and waited.

"Is your heart racing like mine?" Mr. X said loudly from the back of the house. I couldn't tell if he was down the hall or near the other entrance to the bathroom. "I'm enjoying myself so much, it's tempting to leave so we can draw out this game we're playing."

"What a cowardly thing to do," I said loudly as I stepped out from behind my mom's desk and slowly walked across the room. "No wonder you have to kidnap young women to sleep with you."

"I had to do that because you ran away from me!" he snarled.

Just as I was about to step into view of the entrance to the bathroom, I stilled. "You did that because you are nothing more than a pathetic, disgusting man who can't tell the difference between reality and delusion."

Finding courage, I leaned forward and looked in and through the bathroom. When I didn't see him, I quickly moved toward the foyer. I led with my gun as I glanced down the hall. He wasn't there, either.

The sound of something shattering came from the back of the house.

Is he leaving?

I moved back into my mom's office and headed for the bathroom. Walking quickly but quietly, I went through the bathroom until I reached the hall that led to the mudroom and kitchen. When I stepped out into that hall, I'd be able to look slightly right and immediately see inside the kitchen's entrance, while the entrance to the mudroom would be all the way to the right. I'd have to pick one to search first.

Before I moved out of the bathroom, I got the feeling like I was walking into a trap. That him breaking the glass had been his way to lure me out.

I backed up a step, unsure what to do. Then I heard glass crunch in the foyer.

How?

I rushed out into the hall, turned left, walked a few feet, and turned left again to see down the hall toward the front door. To my disbelief, Knox and Creed were standing in my foyer. Knox had his pistol aimed in front of him while Creed held a bat.

"How—" I was so shocked to see them, it was all that I could say.

The moment that word reached them, they looked at me.

Knox took a step toward me and crystal crunched under his foot. Frowning, he glanced down, and that was when I realized the mistake I had made. In my peripheral, I caught movement. I tried to dodge, but I felt the familiar pain of his knife cutting me from the top of my shoulder to my heart.

"Shiloh!" I heard Knox and Creed yell.

Mr. X slashed at me again and I had to hop backward. He went to slash again, and I knew I wouldn't be able to dodge in time. I tried to aim my gun at him, but as I did, Keelan appeared behind him. He caught Mr. X by his wrist and wrapped his arm around his neck, putting him in a choke hold.

Keelan struggled to hold him, and I was too scared to shoot because one wrong move and I could end up shooting Keelan. Colt came out from behind Keelan and grabbed Mr. X's other arm to help. Then Knox rushed to them and took over holding the arm Keelan had been struggling with. Creed came up next to me and I understood what I needed to do.

I gave Creed my gun and I pulled the knife out of my boot. I pushed Mr. X's head back with my palm on his forehead. Keelan adjusted his hold by moving his arm from around his neck and hooking both of his arms under Mr. X's armpits.

"Are you still enjoying yourself?" I asked him as I stared deep into his eyes. His dark depths used to be so terrifying and had haunted me for so long. Something seemed to change. It had to be me, because as I held his eyes, he wasn't my demon or my boogeyman anymore. He was still a monster in a sense, but he was mostly just a man. One that was clearly pissed off. I had a feeling it had to do with who was holding him and the fact that no matter how much he thrashed against their hold, it was to no avail.

I cupped his chin and dug my fingers into his face around his mouth to hold him still. As I pressed the tip of my knife to the side of his neck, I said, "I am not yours. I never was."

Knox leaned his head close to Mr. X's ear and whispered, "She's ours."

Mr. X's nostrils flared, and murderous rage filled his eyes as they rolled to look at Knox. With that one look, I saw what Mr. X wanted to do to Knox—to all four of them if he got free. Seeing that, my own rage took over me. I slammed my knife into his neck, twisted it, and then ripped it out.

Blood sprayed me and Knox and the floor. It spilled out of Mr. X's neck far quicker than it had out of Shayla's and when his legs buckled, my guys let him fall to the floor. Blood spread around him quickly and we all backed away from it.

When I saw Mr. X's eyes go vacant, I felt safe enough to look away.

Not even a minute later, sirens became audible, quickly getting closer.

"I guess Ian finally got my message and called the police," I said.

When EMS arrived, they found Logan unconscious in the attic. He was rushed to the hospital. I got to ride with him because I also needed to go for the large slash that stretched from my shoulder to the center of my chest.

Logan was rushed into surgery as soon as we got to the hospital. The doctors said he had internal bleeding in his abdomen. I was given a private room to get stitched up by a doctor and questioned by the police. I recognized one of the officers and he was familiar with my history with Mr. X.

A few hours passed and my adrenaline had finally crashed. I was alone and lying down when there was a knock on my room door. "Come in!" I called.

The door opened, revealing Keelan, followed by his brothers. I was so relieved to see them that I instantly started crying. Keelan and Colt rushed to either side of my bed. Colt took my hand and Keelan brushed loose hairs away from my forehead. Creed came to stand next to Colt and sat on the edge of my hospital bed. Knox stood at the foot of it.

"How did you know how to find me?" As soon as I asked that, I knew the answer. "You put the AirTag in my car. When did you do that?"

"When Knox and I went to go get dinner the night you took off," Colt said.

"How—"

"When you gave me that speech about wanting to spend the rest of your life with us and wanting babies, Shi," Creed said, cutting me off. "How could we not know something was up?"

Knox gave Creed a look that screamed, *Really?* "You didn't suspect a thing," he told him. Then his gaze flicked back to me. "You had just told us X had Logan. Then I overheard you talking to Creed. You said the reason you told him about the future you wanted with us was so it would help him when he got upset. Meaning something was going to happen to upset him. That and the fact that you only said it to him tipped me off that you were going to run off on your own again."

"That's why you were gone for so long when you left to go get dinner," I said.

Knox nodded, reached into the back pocket of his jeans, pulled out a phone that he must have bought when he'd gotten the AirTag, and showed me how they had been tracking me with an app.

I looked from Keelan to Colt. "How did you two get in the house? The windows and back door were nailed shut."

"There was a broken window in the kitchen. We climbed through there," Colt answered. That must have been the window Mr. X had broken to lure me to him.

"You know," Keelan said, "just because the majority of us are calmer and more collected than Creed doesn't mean that we weren't just as upset that you left."

"Hey!" Creed snapped.

Colt and Knox snorted.

"How mad are you with me?" I asked them.

Creed put his hand on the blanket where my thigh was. "You might not be able to sit for a while. I plan on spanking that ass hard every time I bend you over for the foreseeable future."

That didn't seem like a punishment to me. Not that I was going to tell him that. I wiped my wet cheeks. "I can truly promise to never do something like that again."

"There isn't a reason for you to run off and battle a serial killer by yourself anymore, babe," Colt said.

"Has it sunk in yet that he's gone?" Keelan asked.

I shook my head. "I keep waiting to wake up and realize that this is a dream."

"You must feel something?" Knox asked.

I let out a heavy exhale. "I'm worried about Logan, but I am looking forward to going home and returning to our life. When I let myself think about it and how there won't be this fear shadowing me everywhere, every minute, I feel free and a thousand pounds lighter."

That made them smile.

"So in this future you want, how many babies are we having?" Keelan asked.

I blushed, blindsided by the question.

Keelan's brows rose. "Would you look at that. I didn't even say anything dirty."

Their laughter filled the room, and it was beautiful.

21

EIGHT MONTHS LATER

MY HEART WAS POUNDING, MY LEGS WERE BURNING, AND MY breathing was labored as I slowed my running to a jog around the track on the second floor at Desert Stone Fitness. When I made it back to the stairs, I put my hands on my waist and just focused on breathing for a little bit. I was covered with sweat. I'd pushed myself. Not to escape, but to build up my endurance for a marathon I was planning on doing in a month.

Breathing somewhat normally, I made my way downstairs. I headed toward the front of the gym. Derek was manning the front desk today. He smiled as I approached. "How long did you run for?"

I wiped sweat from my brow. "An hour and a half."

"Nice," he praised. "Just know that I won't hold back in practice even though your legs are sore."

I snorted. Derek had taken over my training a few months ago because every time Keelan and I trained privately, we ended up naked. The only way he and I sparred was in a class setting when I helped him teach. "Don't worry, I'll be fine." I went down the hall behind the front desk and almost ran into Katrina, the assistant manager at Desert Stone, as she came out of her office.

"Hey, girl!" she greeted me as she passed.

"Hi!" I said with a smile and continued down the hall.

Keelan's office was empty because he was in the middle of teaching a class. Colt and Creed weren't here today; they were at home setting up for the party we were having tomorrow. Knox was sitting behind his desk in his office and looked up at me as soon as I entered.

"Isn't it lunchtime?" I asked him.

"I was waiting for you."

"Oh, good." I went around his desk and leaned down to kiss him. "My legs hurt. You can hold me in the shower."

The corner of his mouth twitched. "Who says?"

I kissed him again. "I do." I squeezed his biceps. "It'll be a good workout."

He snorted. "Lifting you isn't a workout." He reached for the phone on his desk and hit the button to call Derek.

The line rang once. "What's up, boss?"

"I'm taking my lunch."

"Enjoy your break," Derek said before hanging up.

I gave room for Knox to go close and lock his office door. "We can make it quick, so you have time to eat," I said.

He took my hand. "I'll eat in the shower."

I couldn't find it in me to argue as he pulled me into his private bathroom. Right away, Knox turned on the water to get it warmed. We made quick work of removing our clothes. Then Knox lifted me by the backs of my thighs. I wrapped my legs around his waist and I kissed him as he carried me into the shower.

He tried to help me wash. He got really distracted when

it came to washing my boobs. Because they were soapy, his fingers and palms slid over them easily and he thoroughly enjoyed the feel of that. I didn't complain, either.

When I was clean, he bent me over and smacked my butt.

"Knox!" I snapped. For the past eight months, ever since Creed had declared he was going to spank me every time he bent me over as punishment for facing Mr. X on my own, all four of them had done it. Every. Single. Time.

It actually wasn't that bad. I found it hot, but after three months of that, I'd started to protest to save face.

He chuckled as he knelt behind me. With his big hands he squeezed my butt cheeks before he used his thumbs to spread me open. I felt his warm breath before his tongue lapped over my clit. Then he licked me from one end of my slit to the other.

"Oh, God, Knox!" I moaned and I put my hand on the wall so I didn't fall over.

His breath puffed against my wet core as he laughed. "There you go calling me a god again."

"I swear, the ego you Stone boys have—"

He cut me off when he buried his face in my pussy and did as he'd said he would. He ate me for lunch.

When I came, my already-weak legs gave out and he had to catch me. As if I weighed nothing at all, he had me against the wall with my legs draped over his forearms.

"Put me inside you," he ordered.

I reached between us to take his heavy, hard cock in my hand. My fingers wrapped around him, and I gave him a few firm strokes I knew felt good before I positioned the head of his cock right where we both wanted him most. I was slick and ready for him thanks to his tongue. He pushed right into me. Needing to hold on to something, I put my hands around the back of his neck.

As he sank into me fully, we both groaned.

"Fuck, you feel so good," he said in that deep growly voice he got every time we had sex. It was like being inside me made him a little bit feral, and he could be a downright caveman sometimes.

He pulled his hips back, withdrawing his cock until he was almost out of me, and then he thrust back in, making me whimper.

As he began to pound into me, I did my best to keep my volume down. Even though his office door was closed, I still wanted to be careful.

Knox's mouth found mine and he seemed to enjoy muffling my moans with his tongue stroking against mine.

I couldn't stop myself from digging my nails into the back of his neck as I felt my orgasm approaching fast. "Don't stop," I begged.

"Why would I stop?" he growled. "I know you're close." He let out a curse. "When your pussy grips my cock like this, Shiloh…fuck, it's the closest thing to heaven."

His words finished me off and he kissed me to muffle my cries. As my orgasm took over my body, I squeezed even tighter around him and that sent him over the edge. I felt him swell just before he spilled himself inside me. I had been back on birth control since we'd returned home, and with Mr. X no longer in our lives, I didn't get stressed enough to get any more late periods.

Knox rested his head against my shoulder as we recovered.

Panting, I said, "Since it's heaven between my legs, I think that makes me the god."

He snorted before he erupted with full-on laughter. Lifting his head off my shoulder, he smiled down at me. "I love you."

"I know," I said, making him shake his head at me while smiling. He leaned in to give me a quick kiss before pulling out of me and setting me on my feet. I put my hand on his heart. "I love you, too."

When we got dressed and left the bathroom, Keelan was sitting behind Knox's desk while spinning a set of keys on a key ring around his fingers. I assumed the keys opened Knox's office because I could have sworn he'd locked it. Seeing Keelan in his gi reminded me of the last time I'd taken it off of him. That was the last time we'd sparred, and Knox had walked in on us, not for the first time. Because the classrooms didn't have locks, Knox had insisted that we *spar* at home. Which was how I'd ended up training with Derek.

Keelan grinned at us. "Sounds like you two were having a fun shower."

Knox gestured for Keelan to get out of his chair. I went over to my gym bag I'd left on the long conference table that took up one side of Knox's office. Next to my gym bag was a large lunch box that held food for both Knox and Keelan. I put the strap of my gym bag on my shoulder and set the lunch box on Knox's desk. "Here's lunch for you both." I leaned down and kissed Knox. "You need to eat more than me for lunch," I mumbled against his lips, making him smile.

Pulling away, I went to Keelan, who was now sitting in one of the chairs in front of Knox's desk. I gave him a kiss.

"I'm heading to the store before heading home. Let me know if you need anything."

"You better hurry," Keelan said. "Don't you have therapy with Logan in a few hours?"

Logan had thankfully survived his surgery and made a quick recovery. He'd taken more time off of work and moved here to Arizona. He currently lived in my house. Well, my old house. For the first couple months after I'd killed Mr. X, he'd surprised the heck out of me and started therapy. He'd really worked on healing himself and when he'd been ready, he'd asked me if we could do therapy together to help fix what grief had damaged in our relationship. I'd happily agreed and I never missed a session.

"I'll make it in time," I said. "I have to pick up last-minute things before the party tomorrow."

"If you tell me what it is, I can pick it up on the way home," Knox said. "You shouldn't have to do so much work for your birthday."

"I'm not just buying party stuff, I'm buying things for our house that we still need. The guest bathroom doesn't even have a shower curtain," I explained as I headed for the door.

"By the way," Keelan said just as I opened the office door, "I think this hair color is my favorite."

I looked down at my wet lilac braid. One year ago, I had dyed it this color. Yesterday, while at the salon with Isabelle, I'd decided to dye it back to purple. "I thought you loved my red hair."

"Don't get me wrong, you're sexy as hell with red hair. When you came over after you just dyed it red, wearing that little black dress..." Keelan blew air through pursed lips while shaking his head.

"It was torture," Knox said as he opened the lunch box.

"That's because you were being a stubborn ass," Keelan said to him. "I loved you with red hair, but your hair now reminds me of when we first met."

Well, that made me all gooey on the inside. "Have I told you that I love you today, pretty boy?"

He gave me an adoring smile. "I love you too, baby girl."

The next morning, I woke up without having a nightmare. I had them less and less often lately. As I glanced around an unfamiliar room that still had boxes in the corner, I had to remind myself where I was. This was our new house. It was our fourth night sleeping here. I was safe between two of my gorgeous boyfriends.

After we'd returned from Maryland, I'd practically moved in with the guys. My house had become tainted by Mr. X and it had been weird having any of my guys spend the night with Logan living with me.

About four months ago, I'd sold my house in Maryland. It had sold quick, despite the murders and dead bodies Mr. X had brought into it. Speaking of dead bodies, Cassy's body had been found in Shayla's bed. Mr. X had really believed she and Shayla were alike and him putting Cassy's body in her bed had been his way of insulting her. The thing was, Shayla hadn't been around to insult. So it had only insulted me. My sister had had her faults, like all people did, but she hadn't been like Cassy. Shayla could be catty when pushed and she'd had an attitude, but that attitude was something I'd sometimes admired about her.

After my house had sold in Maryland, Knox had brought

up the idea of selling their house, too, and we'd used the money from both to buy something bigger for ourselves, or at least big enough for me to have my own space. The guys' house had sold right around the time we'd found our new house and we'd moved in all of our stuff less than a week ago.

An arm that was draped over my waist tightened before lips pressed to my neck. "Happy birthday," Colt whispered in my ear.

I grabbed his hand and snuggled closer. "Thank—" I shot up when reality hit. "What time is it?" I leaned over Creed, who groaned at being woken up, to grab my phone. As soon as I read the time on my phone's screen, I yelped, "I over-slept! I have so much to do before people arrive." I crawled over Creed, who let out another groan. I scurried out of my room like a wild woman and went downstairs to the kitchen.

Knox and Keelan were already awake and drinking coffee at the kitchen island. They stilled and followed me with their eyes as I came running in. I beelined for the oven and preheated it to the temp I needed it at. Then I rushed to the fridge and began pulling out ingredients.

"Shi, baby," Keelan said as he got up from where he'd been sitting.

"What?" I said frantically as I rushed to the other side of the kitchen to pull out my mixing bowls.

As I opened the cabinet and pushed up to my tiptoes to reach them, Keelan asked, "Not that we aren't enjoying the view, but why are you naked?"

I turned to face him with a mixing bowl in each hand. He was standing behind me. I glanced down at myself and sure enough, I was completely naked.

Colt and Creed had woken me up at midnight for what

they called *birthday sex*. It had been a good way to start my birthday and I'd finally cashed in my win from the mud run from last October.

I'd been riding Colt's cock, high on lust, when I'd begged them to fuck me at the same time. Creed had been all for it. It was no secret that he had been doing his best to make me comfortable with the idea of trying anal. Well, I'd finally let him take that virginity last night. They both had been so patient and gentle. When he'd finally had me ready and worked his way inside me, I'd lost my mind. As they'd both rocked into me, they'd whispered dirty things to me, and I'd nearly blacked out coming. Right after, they'd both taken me into a warm shower, where they'd washed me and kneaded my muscles. I'd been so tired and relaxed afterward, I hadn't bothered getting dressed and just gone right back to bed.

Just thinking of last night now was making me blush, but I was sure Knox and Keelan thought I was blushing because I was naked.

"She didn't realize," Knox said as his eyes trailed down my body.

"I overslept and have so much to prepare before guests start arriving," I explained.

"You probably overslept because of all the sex you were having last night," Keelan grumbled.

He sounded left out. I glanced at the time and convinced myself I could spare a few minutes. I set my mixing bowls down and then tried to kneel in front of Keelan.

He quickly grabbed me under my arms, stopping me. "Whoa, baby girl. Today isn't about me." He lifted me up and set me on the edge of the island. With a gentle push, he made me lie back. He put my legs over his shoulders and buried his face between my legs until I came screaming. Knox sat there and watched, knowing that it added to the experience for me.

I managed to get everything I needed done before the party. Currently I was finishing up getting ready. I was wearing a cute navy-blue summer dress. Underneath, I had on my favorite Superman bra and panty set, which had not been taken by Mr. X because they had been in Keelan's laundry basket at the time. The underwear that Mr. X had taken had never been found. For a while, I hadn't been able to bring myself to replace the ones he'd stolen. I had been worried that if I did, wearing them would be a reminder of him. With the help of Dr. Bolton, I'd over-come that worry, and I'd rebuilt my superhero and villain lingerie collection.

I put my lilac hair in a high ponytail because it was scorching outside and I planned to help Knox grill in our outdoor kitchen. The backyard we had could give the guys' old backyard a run for its money. That could just be me being biased, though. It was meaningful and special to me that this was *our* home and I dared to hope that we'd make many wonderful memories in it.

As I was getting ready to leave my room, I saw some-thing in one of the boxes I still needed to unpack. I reached inside and pulled out a framed picture of me, my sister, and our parents. The box was apparently from my old house in Maryland. When I had been in WITSEC, I hadn't been allowed to have any pictures from my old life. Logan had allowed me to have a few on my phone, but it hadn't been the same. Staring down at the picture, I debated where I was going to hang it.

"There you are," Creed said as he and all three of his brothers came into my room.

"People have started to arrive," Colt announced as he came to stand by me.

Creed went to go sit on the edge of my bed while Keelan lay across it. Knox stayed by the door and leaned against the frame.

"Just Ethan and Isabelle," Creed said.

Speaking of those two, they knew the truth about me. When we'd returned, the guys had gone with me to the hospital to visit Isabelle. Ethan had been there the day we'd visited. The guys had stayed out in the hall explaining everything to him while I'd gone into Isabelle's room and told her. Then I'd apologized over and over again. She'd told me right away that what Mr. X had done to her wasn't my fault. She'd been a little sad that I hadn't confided in her, but she'd also understood why I hadn't been able to. Ethan hadn't been as understanding at first. He'd been mad at me and the guys. His girlfriend had almost died, and we understood why he'd been angry about that. But as Isabelle had physically gotten better, Ethan had eventually forgiven us.

As soon as Isabelle had been released from the hospital, she had gone right into therapy to deal with what she had endured. Mr. X had stabbed her ten times and she now had scars just like me. She was still working through her trauma, even to this day. Scars were not easy to bear. Especially how she'd received them, and because of that, Isabelle and Ethan's relationship had been a little rocky. I was optimistic their relationship would persevere, though. Either way, it was Isabelle's story to tell.

I set down the picture of me and my family on my dresser next to my diploma from Copper Mountain High School. Colt seemed to spot the diploma and picked it up to look at it. He was clearly reading my name on it. My real name.

"Did you finish getting everything changed back to McConnell?" he asked as he set the diploma back down.

"Yes. Finally." Now that I was no longer in WITSEC, it had been extremely time-consuming to un-erase myself and take back my true identity. Logan had called in some more favors with his ex-SEAL buddies to help with the un-erasing part. I'd tackled the mountain of forms I'd had to fill out to change my name back for everything.

"It won't be as difficult the next time you have to change it," Knox said.

I turned to look at him. "Next time?"

They all smiled.

Colt sighed. "I guess we could give you a few years to be a McConnell again. That way all the hard work you put into changing it back doesn't go to waste."

"We should give her until she finishes culinary school," Keelan said.

I was about to start culinary school soon while Colt and Creed went to the university nearby for business. One day they wanted to expand Desert Stone and wanted to have the education to do it. They seemed excited about it. Therefore, I, Keelan, and Knox were fully supportive.

"I think we should have her change her name in a year," Creed grumbled.

I looked from one brother to the other and smiled. "And what will I be changing my name to?" I asked even though I had a feeling I knew the answer.

"Stone," Knox said.

"Shiloh Stone," Keelan said as if testing out how it would sound.

"Chef Stone," Colt said. "It has a nice ring to it."

"She'll be Mrs. Stone," Creed said.

The room fell quiet and they stared at me, waiting for me to react.

I smiled adoringly at all of them. "You can ask me whenever you feel the time is right."

A throat was cleared. "Where's the birthday girl?" Isabelle's voice said from behind Knox. "More guests have showed up. One of them said they were your cousin, Micah. He's here with his friends and Shi's uncle is here, too."

Knox glanced at her over his shoulder. "We'll be down in a minute."

Creed and Keelan stood from my bed. "Time to celebrate your birth, Shi," Creed said as they approached.

I took in all four of them, feeling happy and content. "Have I told you four that I love you today?"

They all said yes. Colt took my hand and the five of us headed downstairs.

"You're welcome to say it again, baby girl, but then I'd make you late for your party," Keelan said.

"Didn't you get enough of Shiloh's love this morning on the kitchen island?" Creed grumbled.

Keelan sighed dramatically. "It was the best way to start the day."

I shook my head, smiling. "Dirty Stone boys."

The End

MORE BOOKS BY ASHLEY N. ROSTEK

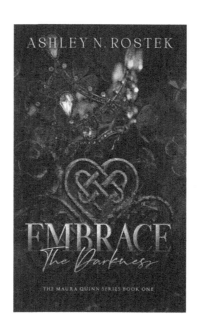

The Maura Quinn Series

Turn the page to read the first chapter.

22

EMBRACE THE DARKNESS

CHAPTER ONE

"SHIT! SHIT! SHIT!"

Attempting to calm myself, I relaxed my white-knuckled grasp on the car's steering wheel and I took a deep breath. When that didn't work, I pulled at one of the many rubber bands around my wrist. *Snap!* The slight sting always anchored me, temporarily pulling my focus.

I was mentally kicking myself for forgetting my flash drive—the one thing I'd needed to make sure I'd had before I'd walked out the door this morning. It held my slide presentation for my afternoon psychology class, which was going to start in thirty minutes. The majority of my grade was depending on that damn presentation, and of course, the professor had to be a stickler when it came to punctuality and liked to lock the door as soon as class started.

Stressed and pissed off were the worst kind of combination. It made it harder to keep what I called my *darkness* at bay. *Just breathe, Maura. Reel it in.* Easier said than done. *Snap! Snap!* My poor wrist was going to be sore by the end of the day.

Driving more than ten miles per hour over the speed limit, I pulled up to the little townhouse community, located thirty minutes outside of Trinity College, which I'd managed to cut down to twenty. I whipped my black Audi into my reserved spot like a bad stunt driver and paused when I noticed my boyfriend's Jeep parked in the spot next to mine.

He was supposed to be at work.

Tom, my boyfriend of just a little over a year, had started working at a law firm downtown. Things had been moving along great for him there. His boss had assigned him his first case, one that'd been demanding a lot of his time, especially his nights and weekends. I'd never admit it out loud, but I was kind of relieved he was so busy.

Tom had graduated last May. The summer off together had been nice. When I'd had to return to school this fall, he'd been bored at home, still looking for a job. Our relationship had become... strained. My first three weeks back in class, all we'd done was fight. He'd wanted attention and thrown fits when I couldn't give it to him. I was working on my master's in behavioral psychology and the workload was atrocious. Tom had not been understanding of that. Instead, he'd made a point to make me feel guilty that my every waking minute of every day hadn't been dedicated to him.

Sighing, exhausted by the memory, I tried to remind myself it had been a difficult time for us both. The universe had decided to grant us a reprieve when he'd been offered his dream job. He was busy. I was busy. Things were better.

Despite his faults, Tom could be sweet and charming, and had that sexy intelligent appeal. He was kind of nerdy, with his goofy thick-rimmed glasses and mud-brown hair parted down the side. He loved to research old court cases as a hobby and watch Law and Order just to point out the mistakes. It was adorable. The good outweighed the bad. That was how things were supposed to be. Nobody was perfect... right?

The best of all his attributes: he was normal. He came from a normal family. He lived a normal life with normal thoughts and aspirations. Just being around him made me feel normal, which was something I'd wanted for a long time.

Was I getting tired of saying the word *normal*? Yes. I honestly hated the stupid word more days than not lately, but it was what I needed. It was what I'd dedicated the last six years of my life to maintaining. *There's no going back.*

I jumped out of my car with my house key at the ready. In my pursuit of the flash drive, I rushed through the front door and dropped my purse on the coffee table in the living room before dashing up the stairs and heading down the hall straight to our room. I was so focused on grabbing my flash drive and leaving as fast as I could, I didn't really pay attention to my surroundings, or else I would have noticed right away something wasn't right.

I beelined for my nightstand, where I'd put my flash drive the night before. From the bathroom connected to our room, I heard the shower running. *Tom must be in the shower*, I mused as I shoved the small black drive into the front pocket of my jeans. Because I was in such a rush, I debated whether I should just leave without saying a word to him or poke my head into the bathroom to say a quick *hi* before rushing back out the door. I decided on the latter. If he found out I'd come and gone without caring to see him, I'd never hear the end of it.

Be more caring and understanding, Maura.

Tom was a sensitive man. Not saying I wasn't. It was

just, lately... I'd been trying very hard to ignore the fact it sometimes felt like a chore to have to be understanding toward his feelings. For the hundredth time, I reminded myself Tom was different. He was a good man, a normal man, even if he could be a big man-baby sometimes. He was extremely different than the men I'd grown up with, that was for sure.

Stop thinking about them. They're your past, not your future. Tom is your future. I had to stop comparing my life now to what it had been before.

I shook my head to clear the unwanted thoughts before heading toward the bathroom door to get my, "Hi, sweetie! Bye, sweetie!" over with so I could drive like a madwoman back to campus.

Reaching out to push open the door, I paused. *What the fuck?* The sound of a feminine giggle slammed into me like a semi-truck. Standing a few feet from the door that was slightly ajar,

I was close enough to hear what exactly was going down in my bathroom.

When I heard the woman moan, my stomach plummeted. I backed up, stepping on something in the process. My unblinking eyes dropped from the door, finding my feet surrounded by clothes that had obviously been thrown askew. A sleazy red bra and matching lacy thong that were definitely not mine, along with the suit I saw Tom wearing this morning before he supposedly left for work. *What the fuck?* I mentally repeated.

"Oh, Tom! Right there!" the woman cried out.

I know that voice!

The knife of betrayal sunk a little deeper into my back. I was almost certain it was my friend Tina's voice. We'd been friends for five years, ever since we were dorm-mates sopho-more year. Sure, she was a bit of a wild card and objectified men like they existed for her enjoyment alone, but I'd always liked that about her. She was fun and had always been a good friend to me. In the beginning of our friendship, she'd patiently coaxed me out of my shell, helped me adjust to a normal way of life, which in turn had prepared me for Tom. Hell, she'd encouraged me to date him!

I never would have thought she'd... We'd just had lunch yesterday. The entire time I'd vented about mine and Tom's problems and the bitch had just sat there pretending to be my friend while giving me advice.

I took another step back, trying to mentally remove myself from what was happening. I needed a moment to process everything. My emotions were threatening to take over and letting that happen was never wise.

My father's voice echoed in my head, warning me not to chase the rabbit. Stay in control.

I took a deep breath to collect myself. Once I had most of my pressing emotions locked up, I tried to think of how I was going to handle this.

Should I barge in there and watch them flounder at being caught? Should I go downstairs and wait for them to finish? Or should I go to class and pretend I didn't see anything? Pretending seemed like the easiest and most appealing option, but what did that say about me? Could I really look the other way? I'd never been the type to allow others to walk all over me, so why was I okay with it now?

Damnit! I don't know!

The water in the bathroom shut off, interrupting my internal debate. My eyes darted around the room, catching on the door to my walk-in closet. It was the closest place I could get to as the bathroom door started to open. I dashed into the tiny room, regretting it instantly. *The closet, really, Maura?*

I left the door cracked, giving the windowless room a little light. Apparently I was a glutton for pain, because I couldn't stop myself from peeking out as Tom and most definitely Tina stepped out of the bathroom. *You don't want to see this,* I told myself, but I couldn't look away.

They were both naked, dripping wet from their shower. I watched my boyfriend carry my friend with her legs wrapped around his waist. Their lips were glued to each other while their tongues played tonsil hockey. One of his hands slid between them, making her squirm in his arms.

Unable to remove my gaze, I couldn't help but compare what they were doing with what he did with me. The way he touched her, his fingers between her legs. I knew how those fingers felt, soft but firm as he stroked my sensitive flesh.

I think I'm going to be sick.

He threw her on the bed, amping up their foreplay to rough passion, then climbed over her and thrust little Tom between her legs. I covered my ears as she gave a gag-worthy performance by screaming out his name before they started going at it like rabbits.

The sounds made me feel like I was trapped in a bad porno. His grunting, her moans, and *my* bed shaking was worse than listening to someone scratch a chalkboard. I stepped away from the door in a futile attempt to put space between us.

Less than five minutes later—I assumed, because I knew from experience he couldn't hold out very long—the noises subsided. I peeked out again to find them cuddling under the bed's sheet.

"When will Maura be home?" she asked.

Tom leaned over to read the clock on my nightstand. "Not for another four hours. Her afternoon class is about to start."

Fuck! I forgot! This day was getting shittier and shittier.

"Good. I get to have you for a little while longer," she purred as she leaned in to kiss him affectionately. "Have you thought over what we last discussed?"

He sighed. "I need more time."

His response was apparently the wrong one. Tina jerked away from him, sitting up abruptly, causing the sheet hiding her breasts to fall. *Fake breasts!* At least mine were real; not as big, but they were nothing to sneeze at.

"I don't see how hard it is to just leave her, Tom! You can't stand her. The thought of having sex with her is a turn off because she's been milking the victim card. Which, I honestly think she's lying to get attention. If she was really raped, shouldn't she be over it by now? It's been seven years. Like, get the fuck over it already."

My breath hitched, my lungs constricting. *He told her?*

"Listen, Tom. Maura isn't what you signed up for. She's a frigid bitch with some serious mental issues, and if she *is* even telling the truth, that pussy is damaged goods. You need to end it."

My spine went ramrod straight. For years, I'd been working to close the wounds that horrible night had left behind. It hadn't been easy. Most of the time it had felt like a never ending uphill battle. I was still healing. I still had cracks where the gaping wounds used to be. Hearing her cruel words… it was like her boney fingers slipped through my cracks, ripping me open to expose all my pain and insecurities.

I trusted them! I knew there were bad people in this world. God, did I know. But there weren't supposed to be any in this new life I'd made for myself. Everything was supposed to be *normal*!

Was the universe trying to tell me that I was doomed to only know bad people? My assumptions and expectations about this life were just blown to smithereens by two people I thought cared about me. *Yeah, I think the universe just made my fate perfectly fucking clear.*

He sighed again. "I know. You're right."

My whole body started shaking. *How did I let this happen?*

Everything in me hurt. My chest burned with anger, but above all, my entire being—my soul—felt exposed.

The battle going on inside of me was making the walls of the small closet close in and the air nonexistent. I was having a panic attack. I'd had a few in the past, so I recognized all the signs. The best way to stop it was to regain control. I tried to grab ahold of said control, through the black hole of my overwhelming emotions, only to have it slip through my fingers like sand. I couldn't get a firm grip, not with the constant reminder in the other room.

Then get rid of the reminder, my darkness whispered from deep, very deep within me.

No! I shook my head violently. *I can't go back.*

The pain intensified in my chest. Sweat beaded on my skin, plastering my hair to my neck and face. Temptation slithered inside me as my panic attack worsened. My darkness rose and rose as my will faltered. I shouldn't have given in, but I was helpless to stop it. Enveloping me like warm water in a bath, the darkness consumed me, breaking to the surface.

I didn't know how much time had passed. A minute? Two minutes? I wasn't sure, but the change in me was fast.

A strange calmness took over, banishing the attack that had wreaked havoc on my body. It felt like a different *being* controlled me with its own thoughts and feelings. Except it wasn't a different being. It was me—a part of me—the darkness I'd suppressed for so long in my attempt to be normal. Now, the seal was broken.

As I reached for my gun safe on the shelf, I found myself numb. There was no internal debate or unsettled feelings with what I was about to do. Just purpose. The gun had been a gift from my father before I'd left for college, as a means to protect myself. I entered in the safe's code and pulled out a sleek silver pistol and matching silencer. The silencer had been a gift from my father's enforcer, Jameson. My family was... complicated.

I screwed on the silencer as I listened in on what was going on in the other room. Tom was talking about going downstairs to get something, then teased Tina about *round two.* I scrunched my nose.

I peeked out to see Tom leaving the room in only his boxers. Tina was laying on her stomach, playing on her phone. Her back was to me, which was giving me a direct view of her skanky ass.

I pushed open the closet door soundlessly and stepped toward the bed. The floor creaked beneath my foot. The sound wasn't loud but still pierced the silence like a bowling ball tossed through a china shop.

I froze.

"Back for round two, baby?" she teased, turning around. Her eyes widened when they met mine. I was too quick for her to react in any other way. Raising my gun, I struck her as hard as I could across the temple. Her body flew back on the bed, unconscious, blood trickling down the side of her face. I took a seat next to her legs on the bed and waited.

Tom had a smile on his face and a bounce in his step when he returned.

Until he saw me.

His smile fell as he stood frozen in shock. He noticed my gun before his focus shifted to Tina behind me. Fear took root in his light brown eyes. He lifted his hands, palms out. I knew he was going to try to *explain,* spewing nothing but excuses. It was what any cheating, lying bastard would do. What he didn't know was that he was already dead to me. He opened his mouth to speak; I took aim just like my father had taught me and shot him in the knee.

He yelled out in pain, falling to the floor. Time ceased as I stood to make my way over to him. I didn't rush, even though I probably should have with how loud he was being, but I couldn't bring myself to move any faster. I wanted him to suffer.

If I hadn't been so pissed off, it would have been comical the way he was rolling on the floor, cradling his knee, writhing in pain. I used the toe of my boot to push him onto his back and held him there. I aimed my pistol again, then started emptying the clip into his groin, pulling the trigger over and over again. His body jerked beneath my foot, his screams filling the room. I kept pulling the trigger, counting each release until I was down to the last bullet. I put that into his head.

The screaming came to an abrupt stop, but it still rang in my ears. I glanced over at Tina. Still lying there unconscious, her chest rose and fell with even breaths.

With empty pistol in hand, I walked back to the bed, only

slowing to scoop up the silk tie Tom had been wearing that day off the floor. I set my gun on the nightstand next to the bed before I rolled Tina onto her stomach.

I climbed onto the bed to straddle her back, pinning her arms beneath my legs. Wrapping Tom's tie around her neck twice, I got a good grip and pulled it tight with all my strength.

She came to when her airway was cut off. She thrashed beneath me. I pulled the tie even tighter, until my muscles burned and my arms started to shake. She struggled longer than I'd thought she would.

Long after her body stilled, I released my hold on the tie. With labored breaths, I climbed off of her, grabbed my gun, and calmly made my way downstairs.

Get your copy of Embrace the Darkness on Amazon

ABOUT THE AUTHOR

Ashley N. Rostek is a wife and mother by day and a writer by night. She survives on coffee, loves collecting offensive coffee mugs, and is an unashamed bibliophile.

To Ashley, there isn't a better pastime than letting your mind escape in a good book. Her favorite genre is romance and has the overflowing bookshelf to prove it. She is a lover of love. Be it a sweet YA or a dark and lusty novel, she must read it!

Ashley's passion is writing. She picked up the pen at seventeen and hasn't put it down. Her debut novel is Embrace the Darkness, the first book in the Maura Quinn series.

KEEP IN TOUCH!

You can find out more about Ashley and her upcoming works on social media!

**MY FACEBOOK GROUP
THE INNER CIRCLE ~ ASHLEY N. ROSTEK'S
BOOK GROUP**
https://www.facebook.com/groups/arostektheinnercircle/

(THE BEST PLACE TO STAY UPDATED)

Facebook
https://www.facebook.com/ashleynrostek/

INSTAGRAM
@ashleynrostek

Made in the USA
Las Vegas, NV
24 January 2025

16939447R00152